The Largs Mermaid

Book 4 of the Boundary Walker series

This work is fiction; names, characters, businesses, places, events and incidents either are the product of the author's imagination or are used fictitiously, and any resemblance to any actual persons, living or dead, events, or locales is entirely coincidental.

Acknowledgements

Thanks to Mrs Sreenivasan Jayandi (Mrs Pathy), Mr Sheik Alaudin Mohd Ismail for their invaluable criticism and comments.

Thanks to Jim Stewart for the encouragement.

Also written by Deryk Stronach

The Boundary Walker   (Book 1)

Blacker Than Black Ops (Book 2)

Never in Ones   (Book 3)

Trilogy   (Books 1,2 & 3)

Books 1,2 & 3 are available in Paperback, Kindle and Audible.

Trilogy is only available in Paperback.

Contents

The Prelude

Lieutenant Colonel Hamish Hamilton, known to most as Ham, had been 'retired' by General Maxwell. The general had perceived that the peculiar work in MIC, Military Intelligence Cryptids, had sent Ham over the top into insanity. It was true that Ham had talked with his late wives, but in the line of duty, Hamilton had met and talked with Fairies, Elves, Selkies, Kelpies and many others folklore creatures, so the general should not have been that surprised. Ham had the Second Sight, as the Scottish called it, a Boundary Walker. He saw and dealt with mythical creatures worldwide, especially from the UK and, more significantly, Scotland. After his forced retirement, Ham's former immediate boss Jack Drummond gave him a Saint John's Wort pouch to wear around his neck. The small bag dulled Ham's Second Sight and allowed him to live a life devoid of ghosts and late-wives. Could you imagine life with not one but two of your late wives looking over your shoulder twenty-four seven? It would send anyone crazy.

When someone or something killed the general's last remaining Boundary Walkers on the other side of the world, he came to recruit

Ham back into the fold. The general sweetened the deal by making Ham a full colonel and giving him an assistant, Captain Alison Macduff and a bodyguard. Macduff was also a Boundary Walker, but she did not initially know it. Ham realised that Macduff was his replacement and that he would not be allowed to retire until she was up to speed. That seemed reasonable to Ham, but he knew he could only teach her so much; the rest she would have to learn the hard way, feet on the ground, sometimes in the water, and occasionally in the air chasing monsters. At the very least, she had to learn not to be killed by them. That would spoil Ham's retirement plans. Anyway, she was expected to protect the cryptids from the humans and visa-versa, all the while making the humans believe that the monsters were only legends.

The bodyguard came in the form of a retired injured Special Forces Military War Dog, called Major. Major's last injury came while protecting his handler in Afghanistan, and he now sported a fine set of sharp metal teeth and an understandable case of PTSD[1].

Another happy family member was a kitten, a not so little kitten called Princess. The name

---

[1] PTSD – Post Traumatic Stress Disorder.

was apt as she was of feline royalty, and she made it plain that feline royalty meant she was the boss, not unlike most cats, but more so.

During their first mission together, Ham's friend and mentor, Jack Drummond, died, leaving a widow, Janet Drummond. Janet was a Selkie, a seal-human who, by covering herself in her seal skin, became a seal and returned to human form by removing the fur. Janet's human form was pleasing to the eye of any male with a pulse, being an Amazon of very feminine proportions. She looked in her late twenties but was, in fact, over two hundred years old. Selkies lived a little bit longer than humans. Jack's dying wish was that Janet become Ham's wife, but Ham was not happy with that idea. She was his late best friend's widow, and he would not contemplate such an arrangement. Plus, Ham was in his mid-sixties, and although Janet was older, much older, she looked thirty tops; it would look terrible. Macduff encouraged their relationship, Janet wanted it, but Ham was adamant. That battle was not over if the women had anything to do with it. To the women, it was a game, but to Ham, it was an unnecessary distraction.

After Ham's return to duty, several other members joined the team during their recent missions. John Paterson, an SBS, Special Boat Squadron, operator seconded initially to Royal Navy Intelligence before joining the MIC family. Of the two other SBS Operators, Rob Ingram and Jaimie Nichols, Rob was a crusty veteran, Jaimie the junior was the youngest of the 'water warriors. The three had joined the team by accident; they just happened to be at the right place at the right time and were suitable candidates, so Ham took them on board.

The last military member of the team was Steve Ives from the SAS, the Special Air Service. Ives was another Boundary Walker, but as Macduff had been, he was unaware of his gift. He differed from the other operatives in that the general had recruited him from the Regiment to join the team directly—a necessity at the time of a particular mission. SAS training often involved training by the British Intelligence Services. Ham was a little bit wary of Ives because of this, as he knew the British Intelligence Services would love to infiltrate his department and get to know what he and his team were up to, either to use the information or, to destroy what they might see as a potential threat. MI5 and MI6's record of working against other 'secret' organisations was legendary. They even habitually fought against each other, as much as the enemy. Ham was worried that Ives might be a mole, planted by one of the two intelligence services, and he had kept him busy elsewhere whenever contact with folklore creatures was unavoidable. It was getting harder, not to mention troublesome, and Ham knew he had to find a remedy to the situation.

The Summons

Semi-retired Col. Hamish Hamilton, known to nearly all and sundry as Ham, was strolling along the Largs Promenade in the darkening Winter's evening light toward the boating pond in Aubrey Park with his bodyguard, Major. Major, an Iraq and Afghan War Special Forces veteran, was also semi-retired due to injuries received in the line of duty. Major sported a set of metal teeth, the best a grateful military could afford. Amongst Major's many physical and mental injuries, Major's jaw was damaged almost beyond repair defending his special forces handler. General Maxwell, Ham's boss, liked to say that Major, the Belgian Malinois military dog assigned to guard Ham had more medals than his new owner. Ham did not give a monkey's uncle about awards or accolades; to be left alone with his team to do his job, or better still to be left alone in retirement, was all he was after. Those medals that he could not refuse lay in the bottom drawer of his bureau.

Ham wore his habitual Grey fabric Kangol flat cap, olive green Barbour Beaufort jacket, beige cargo slacks and comfortably thick ankle-length boots. Major wore a weather-beaten leather collar with a matching leash. The leash was for show, to keep the general public happy, that such a dangerous-looking beast was kept under control. When Major smiled, the general public hurriedly stepped back in alarm. Unless otherwise ordered by Ham or unless danger threatened Ham, Major was the most friendly and calm creature. To show that he liked you, he smiled. This action exposed a set of metal teeth, more threatening than any fictional Bond villain.

General Maxwell had retired Ham, citing mental health issues when Ham could not operate without seeing and talking to his late wives. Maxwell had later brought him back into the fold of MIC, Military Intelligence Cryptids, a small but highly secretive department, when the other team leaders and their field agents had disappeared on operations in the far reaches of the globe. Sudden and sometimes gruesome deaths while on a mission were not uncommon in the department's history. By the very nature of their job, dealing with fire breathing, blood-sucking, evil, and sometimes just plain bad-tempered folklore creatures made the job hazardous enough without the added danger of a mentally unstable senior operative. Understandable but not desirable.

Nevertheless, Ham had been the only living operator/team leader the department had.

Ham was a Boundary Walker, meaning that he had what the Scottish call Second Sight. This gift or curse allowed him to see people who had died, and sadly when others would die and a few that would not, ever. Second Sight also allowed him to see the true form of the folklore creatures that inhabit the world in the mountains, in the forests, in the lakes, lochs and the seas. Some creatures of legends hid in plain sight in human form, with only Boundary Walkers and other similar creatures able to see what they indeed were. Grandmothers, grandfathers, and especially great-grandparents told stories of Elves, Pixies, Brownies, Kelpies, Selkies, and more. These had become legends and then vague memories. But because one cannot see 'them' does not mean that 'they' do not exist. Ham knew they existed; his job was to protect these creatures from the humans and the humans from the mythical beasts, all the time, keeping these folklore beings in the shadows, hidden from scrutiny and persecution.

The overload of all this information affected how Ham viewed the world. Luckily Ham's former team leader and mentor Jack Drummond gave Ham a pouch of Saint

John's Wort, an herb which, when worn around the neck in a small leather pouch, subdued the Second Sight to a manageable level. Ham only removed the leather pouch from around his neck when needed. This night it hung comfortingly against his chest, keeping late wives and demons at bay.

Taking Major out for his evening walk along the Largs' Promenade, Ham had nearly reached Aubrey Park when he saw a dimly lit short, rotund figure waddling towards him, trailing a reluctant cat on the end of a leash. The Cat-Woman, also known to Ham as the Guardian, but the Guardian of what exactly, he was unsure, smiled and waved to him as she drew closer. Princess, the cat, reluctantly stirred from her slumbers inside the small rucksack Ham routinely wore during his walks. Princess stretched. As befitting someone of her royal blood and status, because she was, in fact, a cat of the feline royal line, Princess decided when to walk and when to be carried. Being cold out, she had decided to be borne by her servant. Sensing the Guardian's presence, her curiosity made her pop her grey-black striped head out of the opening.

"Mr Ham, how lovely to see you tonight. Princess, your Majesty, you look radiant this evening," the Cat Woman cooed in her Afro-Caribbean lilt with a slight curtsy. "Mr Ham, I have been looking for you." Ham groaned inwardly. He still did not know the Cat-Woman's name, so did not know how to address her; he must ask her one day; so, he smiled and waited. Whenever she appeared, it was for a reason, and she would tell him that reason when she was ready. She waited until she was standing right in front of him. Although not tall, he looked down on her.

"Mr Ham, the Queen, wants to talk to you." Ham did not know what to say. What was this woman saying, and if the Queen wanted to talk to him, he was reasonably sure the general would be the one telling him? Puzzled by the statement, he stared down at the small, dark-skinned smiling face with overly bright eyes, bright red lipstick and even in this light, brilliantly white teeth. Ham became aware that she was nodding her head sideways out to the River Clyde. For a moment, he thought she had a nervous twitch or was having a seizure. He stared at her, wondering what to do, help her to a seat, call an ambulance. Seeing his confusion, she continued, "Out there. The Queen." She lowered her voice, "the Queen." She had the look of an elderly aunt speaking to a, as she regarded, a not too bright nephew. A pause and a sigh of exasperation. "Mr Ham, how many Queens do you know?"

"One," he replied.

"Well, she's hardly likely to be swimming around in the water at this time of night, is she?" Ham racked his brain. Slowly the cogs turned. He looked from the Cat-Woman to the river and back again.

"The Mermaid Queen?" he asked.

"Who else? The Queen has called you for an audience. I suggested the shore beside the Pencil Monument, and she agreed. I thought you would be here earlier."

"If I'd known, I would have come earlier," Ham replied, trying, but failing, to keep the sarcasm out of his voice.

"Go now and see what she wants," missing or choosing to ignore the sarcasm in his voice. "If she is willing to talk to you, it is important."

He wanted to ask many questions, but Ham realised they could wait. The Guardian was just the messenger; the Queen would supply the answers.

A Double Summons

The sixty-odd-year-old Ham, he'd given up counting at sixty, walked back along the promenade. Major, off the leash, walked beside him; Princess had returned to her slumbers in the rucksack. Sprightly for his age, Ham's brown Timberland shoes hardly made a sound as he passed beneath his apartment overlooking the Largs Pier. Major had hesitated at the front door before realising that they were not going directly home. He ran after and joined Ham. They walked on past the War Memorial to the long Castle Bay promenade. Although it was late December, it was a pleasantly cool evening, but the sea breeze added a slight chill. Ham buttoned up his Barbour jacket, pulled down his grey cap, and stuck his hands deep into the side pockets, more for something to do with them rather than protect them from the cold. Going to a meeting with a Mermaid Queen in the middle of the night was not the strangest thing he had done during his long career in MIC. Far from it. In this case, it was just another day or night at the office. He had just walked past Cainies Quay when his handphone rang.

"Hamilton, where are you now? I've checked your normal haunts at the park and your place. Where the devil are you? I need to talk to you," the general spluttered in his usual indignant manner.

"I'm heading towards a meeting general; I won't be long. I'll get Macduff to let you in."

"Let me in! Won't be long! A colonel comes straight away when a general says he wants a meeting in the Queen's army. Who are you meeting that is so damned important anyway?"

"The Queen," Ham replied. He did not like the general's tone and was not in the mood to play soldiers with him. Queens outrank generals; sat on his lips. He fought the urge and waited.

"Don't be facetious! How dare you!"

"The Mermaid Queen has summoned me," Ham explained.

"Why?" asked the general.

"I don't know yet. I haven't met her Majesty yet," with a slight hint of sarcasm, which Ham was sure would sail over the general.

"It might be related to something else that is going on. Get Captain Macduff here to let me in out of the cold and report back to me when you are finished." It was not that cold. Ham suspected the general wanted to 'warm' himself with Ham's whisky while waiting. He rang Alison Macduff and told her to get over to his apartment, let the old goat in, and pour a sizeable whiskey to improve his mood.

Ham walked past Bowen Craig, and along the Bowen Craig Walk, to the tall stone Pencil Monument, celebrating the Battle of Largs where the Scots beat the Vikings in 1263. Ham wondered what the general had meant by 'related'.

No Show

Ham waited about half an hour, moving around the area seeking different vantage points over the river. After discussing it with his two hairy companions, he made up his mind. There was no sign of the Queen. Knowing the general would be getting impatient, he walked back to the apartment, occasionally glancing out over the dark river just in case.

Arriving back at the apartment, he found the general in a more pleasant mood. He was always happier with a whisky inside him, mainly when it was not his own.

"Well? What did she have to say?"

"She wasn't there. Bloody waste of my time. I've called Janet and asked her to come over, Paterson too." Maxwell raised his eyebrows but did not say anything. If Hamilton was inviting his team members, the general was sure he had a reason. The general held out his empty glass; Ham gave him the bottle. Ham went to the kitchen to make himself a mug of tea, but Macduff had beaten him to it. She turned and, silently raising her eyebrows, handed it to him. He shrugged in reply, nodded his thanks and went back to see what the old boy wanted. Captain Alison Macduff, his second in command, followed. In her late twenties, Macduff, a fit, well-proportioned, short-haired blond, was dressed casually in faded tight-fitting jeans and a loose grey sweatshirt. Ham had seen her blue padded winter jacket hanging in the hallway, next to the general's beige cashmere overcoat.

"The Royal Navy has been a bit careless; they have lost one of their experimental mini-subs complete with a submariner somewhere in this area. He may or may not be alive, depending on the hull's integrity and if his life support systems are still working. They wasted a lot of time searching on their own before they reported it to the grown-ups at the Admiralty." Ham had seen a lot of naval activity from his window during the day and had assumed it was just training exercises.

"Er, Lieutenant Commander Fischer was not involved in that initial search, was he by any chance?"

"Why, yes, I believe his name came up. Why?" the general looked over his glass.

"Oh, it was just a guess." Ham had crossed paths with Fischer before. "The scientifically brilliant young man has the habit of making the wrong decisions,[2] especially when people are involved. Fischer would be more interested in his submarine and reputation than the trapped submariner." Ham sighed, and the general let it slip.

Just then, Ham could hear the front door open. Janet Drummond and Warrant Officer One Paterson arrived; Macduff showed them in. The general continued, "They, the Admiralty, of course, have not asked for our help, as they do not know that we exist as an official body, but I think we should ask some of the aquatic creatures, like the Kelpies, Mermaids," he looked at Janet, "and Selkies, to help look. All unofficially, of course."

"Do you think the Mermaid's Queen's summons was anything to do with this?" mused Ham aloud.

"When you mentioned her, it was my first thought. We need to get in touch with her. If it's about that or something else, we'll need to ask for her help." He looked at Janet. "Mrs Drummond?" Janet, a tall, brunette beauty with an hourglass figure that showed more hours upstairs than should be legally allowed, smiled sweetly at the general.

---

[2] See "The Boundary Walker" by Deryk Stronach

"I guess I will be going for a midnight swim then," she said. "I'll go get my skin."

"Macduff, you go with her. Janet, start at the Largs Beach near the Pencil Monument and make your way north. Give it a few hours. If you don't find her, come back, and we'll come up with a plan 'B'. John, you go with them as cover. Keep unwanted eyes away."

"What about the others?" SBS[3] WO1[4] John Paterson asked. Paterson, who stood casually confident, was a dark wavey haired male who reminded some of a tall Tom Cruise. Whenever this was mentioned to him, he would flash his perfect teeth and say, "really", in a manner that made many a young ladies knees tremble.

"Let's keep it just amongst ourselves for the moment," Ham replied. "The others are busy on a CQB[5] refresher with the Royal Marines from HMNB[6] Clyde at the Jackton Police Training College. We'll call them if we need them. Go back to the safe house to grab whatever equipment you need and go with the

---

[3] SBS - Special Boat Service, the British Royal Navy's Special Force

[4] Warrant Officer One

[5] Close Quarter Battle – commonly known to the British 'squaddie', soldier, as Fish: Fighting In Someone's House

[6] Her Majesty's Naval Base

ladies. Ok?" Paterson and the ladies left. When they were gone, Ham turned to the general.

"Now you can tell me the rest," said Ham. The general sipped his whisky and looked at Ham over the glass. "You don't get involved, and you don't come up here just for one little submarine and one submariner." Ham sipped his tea which had become tepid. Ham stood up and walked to the kitchen to make a fresh mug; he did not like cups. It would give General Maxwell time to consider what he, the secretive general, would tell Hamilton. Ham knew he would only hear what the general wanted him to know, somewhere between the truth and not the whole truth.

The most significant decision of Ham's mind at that moment was whether to pop the mug into the microwave or make a new one, decisions, decisions.

A Drop in House Prices

"Nuclear powered mini-subs! You have got to be joking. Whose bright idea was it to test nuclear-powered mini subs in the Firth of Clyde? Fischer's? A genius he may be, but that guy is a public menace."

"Well, all the other tests had gone quite well," the general replied nonchalantly. "It was not only nuclear powered but stealth. They had to test that as well."

"Well, it seems the stealth works so damned well, they can't find it. And stop referring to it in the past tense. If you've lost a nuclear submarine in the River Clyde and it contaminates the area, there will be Hell to pay. I live here, and I have no intention to grow a second head. And it will affect the value of my property!"

"I didn't lose it; the Royal Navy did," the general said with a pout.

"Let's see what Janet can do. If the Merfolk have found your submarine, maybe the Navy can salvage it without too much trouble. I hope that is why the Queen wants to speak to me. If there is another reason, perhaps we can get her to help. I've never dealt with her before.   I've met the King, Edmund, if I remember correctly, and he seems a reasonable fellow. I hope she is the same. Not sure of her name, Maude, I think." Ham shook his head as if it was a non-important piece of information he wanted to get out of his head.

A Night's Swim

As John arrived at the street where Macduff and Janet had their safe house, he checked the area. Deciding that there were no threats, he stepped into the shadows, took out his phone and made a call. Softly he said that he was in position. A few minutes later, Macduff came out, looked about and then led Janet down the road towards Castle Bay and the Pencil Monument. After a while, John followed. He would stare into the shadows and randomly check behind. It was a quiet late December Largs' night, dark and moonlit.

When they arrived at Largs Beach on the far side of the Pencil Monument, Janet and Macduff walked down near the water's edge. As Macduff scanned the dark surrounding area, Janet stripped off her clothes. Naked, she took a seal's skin from her rucksack. This skin she wrapped around herself. Her form changed to a large seal lying on the beach a moment later. There was no grunting or groaning, no creaking of bones or muscle, just a quiet transformation, nothing at all like the dramatic Hollywood special effects. Janet, the tall well-proportioned woman, became Janet, the seal. Janet was a Selkie, a creature able to transform at will between the human and seal form, provided she had her skin.

Macduff bent down and stuffed Janet's clothes into the rucksack and patted the seal on the shoulder or thereabouts. It was difficult to tell where the shoulders were on a seal.

"I'll wait for you here. Good luck." Janet heaved her body around and flopped into the water. Ungainly on land, she disappeared swiftly into the waves. Macduff looked around and, sighting a boulder, made herself comfortable. John Paterson, lying in the tall grass, waited, watched through the night vision goggles and listened. They were alone.

About an hour later, Janet flopped hurriedly out of the water with much commotion. Only when her whole body was well out of the water did she come to a halt. Macduff rushed over to her. As she drew close, she could see the scrapes and cuts on Janet's body. Macduff drew her Glock 19 pistol and, kneeling, cocked and aimed it in the general area where Janet had just emerged. A voice came over the water.

"Tell Colonel Hamilton, when I summon someone, I expect them to come in person and not send some lackey, especially a Selkie."

"Colonel Hamilton did come here, but you were not here. That is why he sent the Selkie to find you. He will not like it that you attacked one of his people. This Selkie is Hamilton's woman." There was a pregnant pause.

Janet, who had transformed back to human form, whispered, "I think Ham might disagree with you about that." Janet smirked humorously and sat up. She groaned and gingerly touched her battle scars. "Damned Mermaids," she muttered.

Macduff holstered her weapon and helped Janet to her feet. A little unsteady at first, she regained her composure and, after drying herself, quickly took her clothes from the rucksack and started to dress.

"Tell Hamilton to go to the end of Largs' pier, and I will talk to him there. It was not my intention to attack the Selkie; my people thought she had come to attack me. They were a little… overprotective."

"Overprotective, my arse," muttered Janet. "I'd eat her tail if it wasn't so old."

"I will tell the colonel, but he will be upset that you attacked his woman."

"Don't push it,' said Janet quietly.

"Don't push it," called out the Queen.

Macduff giggled and helped Janet up the beach to the pathway. They went to Ham's place as it was nearer. Ham fussed over Janet, telling Macduff to ensure she was safe in the warm shower. Janet could take any cold as a seal, but she was just as vulnerable as the next person in human form. Ham thought Janet did not look too steady on her feet. He told Macduff to patch her wounds with the medical kit in the bathroom and put her in Ham's bed afterwards. Ham caught the glint of humour in Macduff's eye. He chose not to respond. Ham knew that the women thought that Janet should move in with and look after Ham, but for various reasons, not the least because she was his best friend's widow, he thought it a bad idea. Although she was over two hundred in human years, she only looked in her middle to late twenties, she was gorgeous, Ham could see that, but he was not in favour of a romantic or sexual relationship with Janet; he just couldn't.

"See to her first, then report to me what happened," Ham said, perhaps a little too sternly. "Don't worry, captain, I shall sleep on the couch tonight. Not sure how much sleep we'll get tonight anyways."

Janet told Macduff that she could manage by herself. Macduff reported to Ham and the general. She told them what the Queen had said.

"Do you want to come with me?" Ham asked the general.

"No, you go by yourself. Listen to what the Queen has to say. She is expecting you; I would only confuse the issue. I'll wait here. When Paterson returns, he can wait at the end of the pier just in case." On cue, John Paterson arrived.

"All quiet boss, nobody around."

"Hamish," the general whispered, "are you ok to meet the Queen? This business with Janet has upset you." Ham stared back at the general.

"Do I look upset?" asked Ham calmly.

"No, and that is the problem. I know you." There followed a few minutes of staring between the two. The general won.

"I'm fine. Don't worry. I am not about to add regicide to my list of crimes." Ham smiled, and the general nodded. Ham could see that the general was not one hundred per cent convinced, but he seemed to accept Ham's reassurance.

A Royal Audience

Ham waited patiently at the end of the pier. The water was relatively calm for a Winter's evening, so he noticed the odd disturbance in the water out of the corner of his eye. He knew she was there, and she knew he was there. She was making him wait because she was the Queen. After a while, he turned and started to walk away.

"Stop! Where are you going?'

"Home, to a nice mug of tea. You wanted to meet me, but all you seem to want to do is either hurt my team or keep me waiting. I have things to do." He turned and looked down at the pale blue face looking up at him from the water. It was an attractive face, mature yet beautiful in a stylish, refined way. Her hair was black, immaculately coiffured and tied back in a small bun and long ponytail. "You want my help, I want yours, but we cannot afford to play around like this."

"I am not used to people talking to me like this," she said flatly, her bright green eyes flashing.

"Your Majesty, I have to think about a young man's life. I don't know what you want, but if we are to help each other, we need to get on with it." She glared up at him.

"You have met my husband, the King," she stated, Ham nodded in reply. "He is a good Merman and ruler." Again, Ham nodded. Ham did not know that, but that was fine by him if she said so.

"Yes?" Ham asked, wanting her to get on with it.

"He has a hobby; I think you call it that. He hunts for shipwrecks." Ham nodded slowly. He wished to goodness that she would get to the point. "It is not so much the wrecks that he is interested in but some of the contents." Again, she paused, but Ham was getting fed up nodding, so he waited, his head still. She had something to say but was reluctant to say it. She continued, "He searches for shipwreck alcohol, particularly brandy, whisky and wine. Many of the bottles lie intact within wrecks. He likes wine old; the older, the better."

Ham was a little puzzled as to where this was all going. Did she want him to supply booze for her husband as a Christmas present? He must have looked confused because she frowned and continued.

"My husband found a wreck. It was carrying crates of brandy. He cannot drink in the water, naturally, so he goes onshore and binge drinks as much as he can. Sometimes he drinks to excess and collapses. He will dehydrate and die if he stays on the onshore too long in Merman form. Find him and get him back to me, or at least back into the water. He has his faults, but he is a good King. And husband," she added quietly. If you bring him back, we will return the mini-submarine."

"You took it? Is the man inside alive? Is he safe?"

"The man is safe for now. The submarine somehow got stuck." Ham would swear she was tutting and slowly shaking her head in mock sadness. I'm sure the craft can be released when you return my husband to me." Ham decided not to ask what would happen if they could not find the King or if he should be found dead.

The conversation carried on for a few moments more, but that was the gist of it; the Queen was blackmailing them into finding and saving her husband, the King. Ham used the time of the short walk back to the flat to form a plan.

As he passed Paterson, he nodded for him to follow.

The Search

"Cheeky cow. Did the Queen say where we should look?"

"She said her people found the wreck and some of the bottles he'd left behind, southwest of the Mull of Kintyre. The Merfolk have searched the sea around that area but need our help to search on land. If he came ashore at high tide and got stuck into his liquid spoils, he could be lying in a dip or behind a rock hidden from their view from the sea. We need the helicopters to look from the west side of the Firth of Clyde, say the Isle of Aran, up as far as the Isle of Islay."

"All the helicopters are up looking for the sub. It will be a Devil of a job getting the Navy to stop that and look for a drunken Mermaid King. How on earth would one explain that one?" Ham had been thinking about this very problem.

"Ok, I'll leave the re-tasking and redeployment of the helicopters to you, as that's way above my level, but I honestly think if we succeed in finding him, we have a better chance of rescuing the submariner. Please talk to whoever you have to talk to in the higher echelons of the Royal Navy. Do your thing, general." Ham thought for a minute. "They could tell the helicopter crews that the search for the mini-sub was a training exercise, that they did a good job. They will search the shoreline for a sailor or marine dressed up in a Mermaid's costume as a reward and final exercise. Whichever crew finds him gets a crate of beer, or rum, or whisky, something like that. They are not to land, but to give a code word so that the others know that they have won, then it is 'Endex',[7] End of the Exercise for everyone else. Bad luck, chaps, try again next time. The crew that finds the mermaid is to fly to Millport, Isle of Cumbrae, where we will meet them at the helicopter pad at West Bay. If it's out of the ferry hours, we'll need transport across to the island."

"I'll arrange that, just in case. Right, so you go back to the King, check him out and if he is alive and well, what then?" asked the general.

"Initially, we check that he is still alive. If he is, we throw buckets of seawater on him, then carry him to the water and hopefully get him seaworthy and sober. I honestly don't know the equivalent of cups of coffee to sober up a

---

[7] Endex – End of Exercise

MerKing. I'm hoping the seawater will do the job. Janet will go and get the Queen. The trick will be getting Janet into the water without any onlookers or the helicopter crew seeing. The Queen is smart enough to stay underwater and not be seen by anyone on the shore."

"Do you think Janet will be fit enough for that? Or that she will want to do that? The Mermaids beat her up pretty badly earlier," said Macduff.

"Selkies heal very quickly; just let her rest for now; she'll be fine. As for the business with the Queen, that was a misunderstanding. I have spoken to the Queen about that. It will not happen again," Ham said. Macduff looked sceptical and raised an eyebrow. Ham looked at Macduff and shrugged his shoulders. "You have to take a royal's word at face value. Anyway, I threatened to put her husband in an Aquarium," Ham added. The general spluttered, spilling his whisky.

"And the submarine?" the general asked, changing the subject.

"We have to take her word that she will release it when she has her husband back. She has no use for a submarine," Ham said with another shrug of his shoulders to indicate that they had no other choice. The general stood up.

"Let me use your bedroom, no, hold on, Mrs Drummonds in there," the general stated flatly, raising an eyebrow. Macduff sniggered. "I'll use the kitchen." He said to Ham. "I have some calls to make, and the language may not be suitable for you, young people's delicate ears. I will need a large whisky," he said to the room generally. As he left the room, he turned and said, "Tell Sergeant Gilchrist that he can come up; he can bodyguard me just as well from here. It's going to be a long night." Ham turned and nodded to John, who got up and left without a word. Ham poured the general's drink. A generous one to keep the old goat happy.

The Wait

It was a long wait; at least it seemed so. At some point, each of those waiting in the flat imagined themselves trapped underwater in a metal coffin. Even Paterson, whose career as an SBS operative was primarily dealing with underwater dangers, pitied the poor sailor. Ham occasionally looked through the spotter's scope he had rigged up on a tripod by his window. He saw the searchlights of some of the helicopters flying along the far shoreline. It was to be a long night. Once or twice, the general's phone rang for various reasons, making the party jump with anticipation. Ham felt helpless. Macduff considered the copious amounts of tea that Ham drank and on the point of suggesting that he get an intravenous drip installed.

Ham's phone rang about ten-thirty in the morning, but it was just SBS Warrant Officer Two Rob Ingram reporting back from the training at Jackton, with the rest of the team, Sergeant Jamie Nicholls and SAS[8] Corporal Steven Ives. Rob explained that they would have returned the following evening, but as Ham hadn't called them, they had decided to

---

[8] SAS – Special Air Service The British Army's Special Force

carry out some night assaults before they left. Ham told them to stand down but not go too far as Ham might need them at short notice.

It was about eleven-fifteen in the morning when they received the code word that a Royal Navy Merlin helicopter had spotted the 'drunken marine dressed as a Mermaid'. When asked how they knew he was drunk, the reply came that he was flat on his back in a rock pool surrounded by half-empty bottles. When asked how they knew he was a marine and not a sailor, the answer came that the marine was flat on his back surrounded by half-empty bottles; a sailor would have drunk the lot.

Gilchrist and the general remained at the flat, while the others got in Macduff's car and took the ferry across to the Isle of Cumbrae. Once there, they circumvented the island counter-clockwise to the helipad on West Bay. The Merlin was waiting for them, engines idling.

As soon as the team boarded the helicopter, it took off. It flew low, skimming the water, heading south-east towards a quiet bay near Garroch Head on the south of the Isle of Bute. Arriving, it circled a couple of times for the crew to find a safe landing spot nearby. The location was remote, and there were no rubberneckers[9]. As soon as the helicopter touched down, Ham, Macduff, and Paterson followed Major as he bounded towards the prone, unconscious King. Ham signalled for the crew to remain with the Merlin as he did so. Paterson arrived after the dog and checked for vital signs when the others came.

The MerKing lay stretched out on a bed of small pebbles surrounded by a shield of larger rocks. His tail shone dully in the sun, like an old fish lying too long on the fishmonger's slab. His upper body was flesh of dull pink, slightly blue hue. His hair and beard were a pale green, matted with a few strands of seaweed. His eyes were open, and the eyes were dry and off white. Things did not look good for the MerKing. Ham looked down at Paterson, who turned his head to face him.

"He is alive but unconscious. I can't tell if it is the booze or the dehydration," reported Paterson. At that moment, the King let out a loud, noisy burp. A toxic gas of old fish and booze sent the team reeling away, gasping for air.

"Sweet Jesus," Warrant Officer Paterson gasped. Even Princess, who had come out of

---

[9] Rubberneckers - Sightseers, 'gawpers'. Those that stand and stare out of curiosity.

the rucksack, was not impressed with the stale fish smell. Major sneezed and looked at the King in a disgusted manner. Ham shook his head, turned away and breathed deeply.

"Ok, let's get some fresh seawater on him, John. Alison, you go with Janet over behind that rock out of sight of the helicopter crew." He pointed to a large rock that stood half in and half out of the water.

"Janet, I've got the Queen's assurance that there will be no funny business this time. Get her and bring her here. We'll get him in the water, so she can get him without coming to the surface." Paterson had already taken the buckets they brought and was filling them in the sea. Macduff and Janet disappeared behind the rock, Macduff reappearing a few moments later alone with a surreptitious thumbs up. Princess sat near the tail end of the merman seemed confused; she looked at the upper torso of the King and smelled the giant fish attached to where his legs should be. Ham shooed her away when it looked like Princess was about to take a trial bite of the tail fin. She indignantly turned her head and studied a crab, trying unsuccessfully to look smaller and inedible. Princess looked purposely away, showing her lack of interest in the proceedings; she did not want a taste of the strange fish anyway.

After dousing the inert King a few times, they carried him in a blanket into the water. He was a limp deadweight. The upper human-like torso was easy to grasp, but the wet, slimy lower fish half was awkward to the point of nearly impossible. They struggled over the slippery rocks. The helicopter crew, seeing them struggle started to come over to help. Ham waved them back.

Ten minutes passed, and there was no sign of the Queen. Ham was getting worried. If she did not turn up and the King was still unconscious, what were they going to do? They could not leave him there, and the longer they stayed there, the higher the chances of discovery by passers-by. Ham looked over at the aircrew, discussing these strange people who had picked up the drunken marine and dropped him in the sea. Was it a man or a manikin? Ham looked down at the King, now submerged just under the surface of the water. A silly childlike smile covered his majestic face; he appeared to be sleeping.

A bark from the sea broke the silence. Ham looked up and saw the seal's head a few meters out to sea. Ham could also see the vague shapes swimming around under the surface near the seal.

"Ok guys, let's launch him," Ham muttered.

"I name this ship the Mermaid King," Macduff replied, and they pushed the sleeping beauty out into deeper water. Ham tapped Macduff on the shoulder and pointed to the rock as they came ashore. She nodded and disappeared, reappearing a few moments later with Janet, wet but uninjured.

They walked back to a puzzled helicopter crew. The crew did not say anything, but they did look puzzled.

"Those bloody Special Forces, they've always got to play games, sneaking around underwater, who do they think they are, bloody Mermaids or something?" John asked, tutting as he did so. The crew nodded in agreement; anyone who joined the SBS was crazy. They all climbed back into the Merlin. They had done all they could; it was up to the Mermaid Queen.

Return to Sender

They were all having a late lunch in the Green Shutters Bistro overlooking the Largs seafront when the general's phone rang. He looked at who was calling and excusing himself; he took the call outside. He returned to join the others. They looked at him, but his demeanour was expressionless. Ham knew the general better than the others.

"So, they found it then?" he asked.

"It just turned up outside HMNB Clyde and sailed in as if nothing had happened. The submariner is fit and well, although more than a bit confused. They'll keep him in the sick bay for a while. He doesn't know what happened. He was cruising along fine and happy, smugly avoiding all detection; suddenly, he was stopped and held fast. He could not move for about forty-odd hours no matter what he tried. Tried everything, he couldn't get loose; he thought he was a 'goner'[10] then suddenly, not only free but rocketing along up the river, faster than the craft's specs[11]. When he came to a halt, he

---

[10] Goner – Slang, someone who is going to die, doomed. They are going to go.
[11] Specs - specifications

surfaced and found himself knocking on the door of HMNB Clyde.

He can't explain it; the Royal Navy can't explain it. So, I think we will leave it that way. I may have to come up with something for the Admiralty brass later, but I suspect a few pink gins, and it will all be forgotten and brushed under the carpet. The Navy are a superstitious lot, so I don't think they would want to know." He sipped his coffee and forked another mouthful of food into his mouth. Gilchrist, who had finished his meal, wiped his mouth with his napkin.

"Shall I get the car and bring it around for you, sir?" The general nodded without looking up.

"Take your time; I need to have a word with Colonel Hamilton." Gilchrist nodded.

"Check that the RAF have the jet ready at Glasgow Airport, would you please, David?" Gilchrist acknowledged, stood up and left the Green Shutters Bistro.

The others just finished their meal, sipped their coffee, drank their water, or crunched on their dog biscuit; it was just another day in MIC.

General Maxwell looked at Ham and nodded outside. Ham followed him out. They walked past the cafe's outside seating area and over to the sea railings on the other side of the promenade. People enjoying the weather would wander past with their families or dog, but they were generally ignored apart from the odd friendly nod.

"I want you to come down to London sometime next week," the general started. "I'm not sure when, but I'll let you know."

"What's it about, sir?" Ham asked, leaning in slightly.

"Can't tell you just yet; some things need to be organised. But I want you to come alone and dress smartly. Civvies[12], not uniform. A suit tie, that sort of thing. You do still have a suit, don't you? You haven't gone completely native. By the way, by alone, I mean alone, especially no dog."

"But I thought Major was there to guard me," Ham pouted.

"No dog. You can guard yourself for one day. No weapons either," he added. The confusion did not show on Ham's face, but he felt it. "A car will take you to Glasgow Airport,

---

[12] Civvies (or civies) – civilian clothing

where an RAF flight will take you down to RAF Northolt. My assistant, Ms Miller, will sort everything out and tell you when. Don't wander off on any adventures. Do what you like with your team, but you stay put. Right? This is important." The general looked seriously at Ham. "Understood?"

"Sir." Ham straightened slightly. "I got it; I got it. But I'm not moving."

"What? Who said anything about you moving?" the general spluttered indignantly, and Ham knew he was on the right track.

"I am not leaving here. You try to move me, and I will resign."

"Yes, yes, quite." Luckily for the general, Gilchrist arrived back. With a shake of the hand, General Maxwell left. Ham noticed that the general did not pay his bill and smirked. Somethings never changed.

To Help a King

During his morning walk, Ham was suddenly disturbed by the familiar lilting Caribbean voice, "The King would like to see you tonight." Ham noted that she had said 'the King would like to see' and not, 'the King commands'. Ham considered that the King might want to say sorry for the trouble he caused or say thanks for the effort, but Ham knew that Kings do not do that sort of thing. On second thoughts, maybe the King was after a favour. Ham nodded to the Guardian in reply. He waited. He looked at her. She looked at him. Ham broke first.

"What's it about?" Ham asked.

"Oh, I think the King should tell you himself. Such a delicate matter," she added in a confidential tone as she leant in toward him. Then the Guardian stood upright, turned and made to leave. As she walked off, she called back, "Do give my love to General Maxwell. Such a nice man." Ham wondered how the cat-woman, the Guardian, and God knew what else seemed to be better informed about what was going on than the protagonists themselves.

"When? Where?" Ham called after her.

"I'll contact you when he's ready. It will be tonight after dusk," came the reply on the wind. "The Queen mustn't know."

What the Hell is going on, Ham wondered to himself? Still, Ham was looking forward to giving the general the Cat-woman's love. He loved to see the old goat splutter. He was still waiting for the general to come back to him about this ever so important meeting. Ham had got his suit out from the suitcase under his bed, ready. It needed airing and ironing with a good steaming to get the wrinkles out. He would have sent it to the dry cleaners, but he didn't know when the general would summon him south. A good hanging in a steaming shower would have to do, followed by a quick press with an iron on a damp cloth.

Around dusk in the winter's evening, Ham stood leaning on the railings, staring out over the dark, glistening, Scottish River Clyde. There was a serenity under the moonlit sky. A gentle chilly sea breeze watered his eyes as he looked not at what lay before him but his past with its places and people. I've had an 'interesting' life thus far, and he thought to himself, judging by recent events that were not due to change soon.

Ham's bodyguard, Major, sat beside him also stared out over the water, motionless except for the occasional twitch of its ears. Both were retired, and both bore scars mental and physical of past adventures. Sometimes Ham wondered what Major thought about when they looked out over the Clyde. Major sported a set of titanium teeth, the originals damaged beyond repair in the battlefield of Afghanistan.

Princess, who insisted on accompanying them during their morning and evening strolls, slept curled up at the bottom of the small rucksack that Ham carried for that purpose. She did not always walk; sometimes, she did not exit the rucksack, but all Hell broke loose if he ever tried to leave her behind.

Next to the dog, Major, another figure stood motionless. Ham liked to go for walks with Warrant Officer John Paterson of all the team members. John knew the value of silence. He did not feel the need the fill the silence with frivolous talk or noise. John, a frogman-canoeist or operator in the UK's Royal Navy's SBS, also had a past worthy of self-reflection. They liked to breathe the fresh air, look at the stunning view and watch the passing people, dog-walkers, joggers, people out for a casual stroll and of course the general tourists enjoying the seaside, even this late in the year.

When Ham had been walking the beasts and checking on the swans, he saw a knee-high toddler by the edge of the Noddsdale Water, a burn[13] which ran along the north end of Aubrey Park. A proud father watched as the child threw stones at a solitary duck paddling happily in the water. "Fook awf dook!" he called out in a squeaky broad Glaswegian accent. A small rock flew a couple of meters away from the unconcerned duck. The little boy had not learned coordination yet. "Fook awf dook!" Another stone flew, landing miles away from its target. The father looked on and smiled. A proud man indeed, Ham thought, shaking his head almost imperceptibly while looking over at the pair of swans, calmly swimming a little further upstream with their cygnets. Swans are beautiful, majestic creatures, but Ham knew they would viciously attack if you piss them off, especially to protect their young. Ham had wondered for a moment if he should say something to the proud father of the 'Fook awf dook boy' but decided that he would just be perceived as an interfering old man and

---

[13] Burn – small stream

walked away, to echoes of "Fook awf dook", splash.

Although John often accompanied the colonel on his evening walks, this evening was not a casual walk to allow the dog to relieve itself before settling down for the night; it was a night to meet a King, initially the King's messenger.

Major stirred. Ham patted his head gently. "Good lad," said Ham quietly.

Princess stirred. Ham turned to look to see who was coming. The Princess did not exert herself for a mere messenger. Who was this Guardian?

The cat-woman spoke, "Good evening Colonel Hamilton, Warrant Officer Paterson, how lovely to see you." The short, round Afro-Caribbean woman walked out of the shadows, this time trailing a reluctant ginger tomcat on a leash. "Don't worry; I shall not detain you too long.

Princess's head popped out of the rucksack opening.

"Meow."

"Good evening, your Majesty," she said to the cat. "How lovely to see you again. I trust you are well?"

"Meow." Ham noticed that the ginger tom stared at the Princess and appeared to bow its head in supplication; after all, a Princess is a Princess.

"Where and when? If it's tonight, I'd like to get on with it and see what he wants."

"Yes, I know," she started. "When you have finished here, maybe you could pop along to the Pencil Monument Pier on the way home. The King will be there." She turned to leave. "Nothing personal, Warrant Officer Paterson, but I think the King would like to talk to the colonel alone. I'm sure you understand." John Paterson did not, but he nodded his head in understanding anyway.

The Guardian turned and left. When she was far enough away, John muttered, "Well, that was a polite way of saying, Fuck off."

"I would never be so crude," came the chuckle from the dark. "And Colonel Hamilton, don't forget to say hi to the general for me." And the voice chuckled into the night.

A Visit to London is Announced

Ham's handphone rang in his jacket pocket. He looked at the caller ID; there wasn't one. His face remained expressionless. How did that woman know?

"Sir." Ham knew who he was talking to, so there was no need to continue with pleasantries.

"Wednesday. The car will pick you up at oh-six-hundred hours. Be smart, and for God's sake, be polite."

"General, I…"

"Yes, yes, I'm sure you will be, but I am just saying. Tomorrow, when you take the dog out, walk south towards the Pencil Monument. Observe the buildings on the way there. We'll talk on Wednesday. By the way, Maddox has been reported in Scotland again. Tell your team to watch out for him." When it came to his moral compass, Colonel Maddox had been Hamilton's American counterpart, not well-liked and someone who suffered from a severe lack of direction. After being removed from the American military, Maddox had gone mercenary or rogue, selling his knowledge and skills to the highest bidder[14]. Ham had thought he had removed the Maddox problem when Shaman Drygeese had erased part of Maddox's memory to safeguard the secret of the Nakanni[15]. Ham considered Maddox like a cockroach, almost impossible to control or eradicate.

Ham turned to Paterson, "John, arrange a team gathering. We need privacy and a bit of space to talk freely. Breakfast is on me. You arrange the time and place. I'll tell Captain McDuff and Janet to watch out for Maddox and his goons; you warn the rest. It's too cold to hang around here; I'm off to meet a King."

"Maddox, boss?" Paterson queried. If Paterson had heard anything from Ham's telephone conversation, he was pretending, very diplomatically, to be ignorant. Ham appreciated the gesture.

"Don't worry about it for the moment. And John, don't say anything about the King to anyone, anyone. Not even the team. Pass the word to everyone when you have the time and venue."

They turned and started to walk back slowly.

[14] See "The Boundary Walker" by Deryk Stronach
[15] See "Blacker Than Black Ops" by Deryk Stronach.

"John, what's your opinion of Ives?" Ham asked casually, but Paterson was not fooled. It was a serious question.

"He's a good lad. Smart, not just intellectually but street smart as well. He looks after his health. Likes to exercise alone, but he's SAS and an ex-Para[16]." Ham quizzically looked at Paterson. Paterson saw this and continued, "Myself and the rest of the lads are SBS, ex-Marines, we are in the habit of training together and fighting together, the Army guys tend to train alone and attack heroically alone." Ham laughed. "It's a cultural thing. He's sociable and gets on well with Rob and Jaimie, especially Jaimie. Jaimie takes him along as wingman when he's out hunting. Rob told me he did well at Jackton, a team player."

"Does he ask a lot of questions about what we do?" Ham asked.

"No, surprisingly little. Just does what he's told and does it well, if you are asking." Ham mused for a while as they walked back.

"Don't say anything. I just wanted to know how he was settling in." Paterson knew it

---

[16] Para – British Army Parachute Regiment

was more than that, but he kept that to himself.

"Of course, boss." They both walked back along the promenade, Paterson peeling off to head for the safe house used by the SBS and SAS men in the team.

A King's Dilemma

Ham had not told the general that he was walking down to the Pencil Monument that evening. It didn't matter, tonight, tomorrow. He would take Major for his walk down there again tomorrow, but a quick look-see would not do anyone any harm. By the time he reached the monument, he had wondered what he was supposed to observe. There was nothing that he had not seen before, the exception being one building, a large red three-storey edifice that had once belonged to a wealthy, probably titled family in days gone by, was having some work done. There was a solid fence hiding the ground floor. These old buildings were constantly being modified, turned into luxury apartments and the like. Ham filed it away in his memory and walked on. Maybe he would see something the next day. He decided to walk Major on the grass nearer the houses and not along the Promenade the next day. He would get a better view of the houses.

As Ham drew nearer to the monument, he scoured the shadows and pricked his ears, listening for anything out of the ordinary. Maddox or his men could have trailed him; he could just as well stumble over a courting couple. A desperate courting couple, as it was getting damned chilly as the night drew on. Ham observed Major, and he did not react, so he knew they were alone.

Ham walked behind the monument and down to the right to the rocky shore. He checked and saw that he was hidden from view to a casual glance from the sea-side houses or strollers on the pathway. He did not have to wait long. Ham saw Major react seconds before he heard the voice from the dark waters.

"Hamilton, it is good to see you again; my wife says you are a good man and can be trusted; I need someone like that." Ham waited, but the King did not continue, so he waited some more. He was about to wait for one last time with mild confusion when the King continued. "The thing is Hamilton; the Queen must not know." Ham groaned inside; what had the old goat done now?

What he had to say obviously bothered the King because he was off on another of his silences again. Ham had met the King before and remembered him being decisive and commanding when sober.

After giving him a polite period, Ham spoke. "You look healthier than the last time I saw you. I'm glad you seemed to have recovered. How can I help you, your Majesty?" Ham could hear and feel rather than see the agitation in the water.

"It's that damned daughter of mine." Oh yes, thought Ham. "She's gone and fallen in love with a fisherman. Not even a damn captain. A common fisherman! The Queen will create a storm if she finds out. I don't know how to deal with her."

"Sorry, your daughter or the Queen?"

"Both!" the King called out in an exasperated tone. "I love my wife, and I dearly love my daughter. In many ways, they are both of the same temperament, calm, serene, loving, but when riled, they are explosive. You know me, I like a quiet simple life. Can you imagine how life would be if those two clash? I need help. I cannot ask anyone in my Kingdom; they will tell the Queen. What should I do?" the King wailed in despair. There was a silence. The King thought that Ham was thinking of a solution. Ham was in a panic; what the Hell did he know about adolescent love? When the King coughed, Ham realised that his time was up, and he had to come up with an answer. First, he needed facts and then he needed details. Lastly, he needed time to think.

"Has she been in touch with the fisherman yet?"

"No." Good start.

"Does he know she exists?"

"Not yet. She observes him from the shadows of the boat and from underwater." Good.

"Which boat and what does the fisherman look like?" The King told him. Ham could tell from the description that the King was not impressed with his daughter's choice of humankind.

"Can you keep this situation under control for a few more days? I need to investigate and think of a possible solution."

"Are you going to kill him?" What!

"What? No. But I'll think of something."

"I could sink the ship," the King said helpfully. "You know, a little accident?" The King had obviously been thinking of his own solutions.

"No, your Majesty, not a good idea. Imagine what would happen if your daughter realised what you'd done. She'd never speak to you again." Dear God, let that be enough to hold him from his homicidal tendencies. "I will come back here in three night's time, four at the latest, with a plan." The King agreed, but Ham could tell from the tone of his voice that a 'little accident' was still on his mind.

Major rather than the King told Ham that the audience was over and they were alone again.

They walked back to the flat. In between shaking his head gently side to side as he considered and discounted various plans, Ham looked again at the buildings. He still could not see what the general had gone on about. Between the King and his homicidal tendencies and the general and his games, Ham wondered if he would ever get a chance to enjoy his retirement.

Indigo Eats

The location John had arranged for the meeting was the Indigo Eats Bistro on the corner of Gallowgate Street and Gallowgate Lane. Entering the caf□ with Major and Princess, Ham looked around, orienteering himself. It was a habit he picked up many years before and had never lost. To the right of the main room, there was a pair of comfy armchairs in front of a pleasant old black fireplace. A warm fire burned in the hearth. But it was up the short flight of stairs on the left that Ham was guided by the owner when he entered. It seemed he was expected. A row of small tables in a fair-sized room, pushed together to form a long table, surrounded by green leather chairs, that could comfortably sit ten customers. There were seven of them, excluding the beasts, so there was plenty of room.

Ham looked around again. To the left was a large window overlooking the street. To the right were the bistro's toilets, men and women, which meant customers might pass through their room at any point. Ham stood in the open doorway and saw no door between the main room and this 'meeting room'. It should not be a problem if they were careful with the volume and what they said. Sometimes, hiding in plain sight was a better security option than acting covert and sneaky. Ham examined the ceiling and noticed the security camera in the corner, another reason to be careful. John saw his gaze and raised his eyebrows. Ham stepped down the stairs and walked over to the manager, a bald chap with a friendly grin. He looked at Ham expectantly.

"Would you mind if we disconnect the camera in the room while we have our meeting? Some of the gentlemen are camera shy." The manager raised one eyebrow, looked through at the tough-looking 'gentlemen', and laughed.

"You help yourself; it's too high for me to reach to disconnect." Ham thanked him and returned to the room, where he pointed to the camera cables and made the gesture to disconnect them. What you know about did not worry you; what you did not was the problem.

Ham took off his rucksack, lay it gently beside his chair, and sat down. A hairy grey and black feline head with sleepy eyes appeared, looked around and disappeared into the comfy warm bottom of the rucksack. When the tattooed waitress came, they ordered breakfast. Ham had a small breakfast, one of everything; Janet declined the food, having already eaten some raw fish at home, the rest had full breakfasts, or rolls with bacon, sausages, eggs and the like. Ham had a coffee in a mug as was his wont, Janet, plain water as was hers, and the rest teas and coffees of various varieties as was theirs. The animals had no choice; Major received a couple of dog biscuits, which after a glance at Ham to check that it was ok to take, he woofed down. Princess, hearing the crunching, poked her head out of the rucksack again, saw what everyone was doing, yawned disinterestedly and disappeared back into her sleeping quarters. Ham had fed and treated her before bringing her out, knowing that she would otherwise try to steal someone's bacon.

Ham was on his second coffee when the rest finished eating. Everyone looked at him expectantly

"Ok, now that you have gorged yourselves at my expense to work." The others leant in conspiratorially. Ham had seated himself so that his back was to the camera, so that anyone possibly viewing the camera footage, even though it was supposedly disconnected, could not read his lips. He knew it was disconnected, but old habits die hard.

"The general has summoned me down to London tomorrow morning, and I'm not sure why. Do any of you have anything you want to talk to me about? Anything at all, no matter how minor." He paused and looked around the room. "I don't like surprises." Ham waited and looked directly at each person individually. Everyone shook their heads. "Maybe, I'm for the heave-ho[17], I honestly don't know." Macduff sucked in air in surprise; the rest sat stoically. "He's always trying to get me to move to London, where he can keep an eye on everything, but he also knows that I am staying in Largs. It's where I choose to be." Ham paused and looked around the faces. "Nobody has any deep dark secrets?" Ham raised an eyebrow quizzically. "Right then, I shall go down and see what he wants. Steve, I would like you to wander into the next-door room, make yourself comfortable with a tea or coffee and monitor if anyone is showing us undue interest." Ives nodded and got up to leave. As he did, Ham signalled for him to lean in. Ham spoke softly saying to Ives, "When I leave, I'd like you to come back, reconnect

---

[17] Heave-ho – to lift, to throw out, to sack

the camera, check with the manager that it's working ok, it got accidentally disconnected, he understands, and join me for a walk along the Promenade. Ok?" Ives nodded, descended the stairs down to the lower room, and found a suitable seat. He ordered himself another coffee and appeared to relax into the role of a young man having a coffee and playing with his mobile phone. Once Ives had gone, Ham gave it a minute and then continued in a quiet tone to the room.

"In the meantime," Ham drew out three envelopes, which he handed down the table to John, Rob and Jaimie with instructions not to open. "These are your missions. How you accomplish the mission is up to you. Use the general's Personal Assistant, Ms Miller, for your needs, you've done it before, you know her number, but you will also notice that there is a very short timescale, seventy-two hours. There may not be enough time to arrange all your needs. Work with what you have. No weapons, no lethal force; these are reconnaissance missions; ideally, you are in and out, and nobody is any the wiser. I want photographs, nothing else. One last thing, you will not, not ever, repeat to anyone, not even each other, what you may see. These missions are of the highest secrecy." Ham looked at their faces. They looked at him, the envelope in their hands and back to him. "You have all been on black ops; I don't mean to belittle those missions, but what I have just handed you is way above that level of secrecy. If any of you succeed and want to talk about what you saw, I'll be available. I don't mean to sound melodramatic, but only those that have completed this mission can ever talk about it to anyone else, and I will decide when, who, and if. Apart from that, keep your phones active until mission time, in case I need you. Leave your phones at home when you go on the mission. One last thing, gentleman, you will see that you are heading for an island; how you manage it is up to you, but I should mention that Great White Sharks use that area as a playing ground. Something to take into consideration when planning your mode of entry." He raised his eyebrows. "Off you go and have fun. Best of luck." The three special forces operators got up to leave.

"Boss, one quick question if I may?" Jaimie asked. Ham raised an eyebrow in an indication that he should continue.

"This, Ms Miller, what does she look like?" Ham saw Rob's eyes roll back in exasperation. Ham's forehead creased momentarily.

"I don't know; I've never met her. Why?"

"Nothing, boss, it's just that she has one hell of a sexy voice." Rob grabbed Jaimie by the scruff of his neck and pulled him towards the doorway. Rob gave Ham a, 'I don't know what to do with him look'. Letting go of Jaimie's collar, Ham saw Rob reach for his wallet and waved his hand away.

"I've got it covered today. You can pay next time." Knowing they never would, they descended the short stairway, waved at the waitress and exited the bistro.

Ham signalled Macduff to come closer and sit opposite him. He leaned slightly over the table and said in a quiet voice to Macduff, "I have an envelope for you too. We both know that Ives is a Boundary Walker and doesn't seem to realise it yet. He needs training and exposure to our business, but I am worried that MI5 or MI6 has gotten to him during his SAS training. MI6 especially seems to think that the SAS is their own recruiting pool. If MI6 has tainted him, we need to know. Go home read the instructions. Contact me if you are unsure of anything and Ms Miller to make arrangements." Macduff looked at Janet, who in turn looked at Ham.

"And me? Where's my envelope?" She seemed to be challenging Ham. He smiled sweetly at her and withdrew an envelope. Unlike the other, this one was not sealed. She held the envelope, noticed that it was not closed, opened it, read it, glared at Ham and called him something which Ham could not hear clearly. He thought it was something to do with his parent's marital status at the time of his birth. Janet showed the note to Macduff, 'Someone has to stay behind and look after the beasts'. The ladies humphed, tutted and shook their heads as if dealing with a problem child. Janet and Macduff left, Janet with a glare in his direction. Ham suppressed a grin; he still was not comfortable showing his emotions.

He picked up his rucksack, scanned the room to make sure nothing was left behind, climbed down the four short steps and walked over to the counter. Major on the leash, by his side, looked hopefully at the waitress with baleful, 'I have not been fed in days eyes', who slipped him a doggy snack. After chatting casually with the staff for a moment, Ham thanked them for the meal, paid the bill, left a tip in the jar, and left nodding almost imperceptibly to Ives.

Huginn and Muninn

When Ives found Ham, he was on the promenade leaning against the railing halfway between Aubrey Park and the RNLI[18] ramp listening to a pair of ravens barking and bickering. Ham seemed fascinated by their antics and rough squawking. As Ives approached, the ravens glanced at, then ignored him. Ham acknowledged his presence but continued to focus on the birds.

As Ham appeared so intent on the birds, Ives moved to his side away from the birds and lent against the railings, waiting for his lord and master to speak. Major sat at Ham's side, watching the birds. Princess was a lump in the rucksack that occasionally meowed and changed position when the birds were too loud.

Presently the birds finished their one-sided conversation and flew off. Ham remained deep in thought for a few minutes, then turned his head slightly to the young SAS corporal and spoke quietly.

"Anybody paying us any undue attention? John warned you about Maddox?"

[18] RNLI – Royal National Lifeboat Institution

Without moving, Ives replied, "No, boss, and yes, boss. Not that I could see. Not here and not in the bistro. Yes, John did warn all the guys in the house."

"Fascinating birds, ravens. Highly intelligent. Did you understand what they were saying?" Ham said, changing the subject abruptly, catching Ives momentarily off guard.

If it were not for the fact that Ham was the boss, and he had asked the question with a straight face, Ives would have laughed in reply. "No, boss, I never picked up the skill." Ham stared for a while at Ives. Ives had been stared at before, but never with the depth that he felt from Ham at that moment.

"You will," was all Ham replied after a while. Ham casually turned and looked around; holidaymakers and dog walkers of various ages strolled up and down the promenade. None seemed to be paying them the slightest attention. He turned back to the river and gazed out at the Largs - Cumbrae ferry plying its trade backwards and forwards. A few yachts sailed casually around, chasing the wind. Ham took his time before he continued.

"Steven." Ives was unsure if being called 'Steven' by the boss was a good or bad sign. His mind raced, wondering if he had done anything wrong. Ham continued, "A couple of things, I've some business to attend to, so I might be away a while. I want you to follow the orders Captain Macduff gives you."

Ives blinked; of course, he would; she is a captain and the boss's right-hand man, or woman in this case, and he a corporal. Strange order, he thought. "Yessir," he replied. Ham did not look at him.

"To the letter, please. I want you to follow her instructions and trust her, ok?"

"Yessir."

"You got a girlfriend, here or anywhere?" Ham asked casually. Ives was caught off-guard again by the sudden change in the conversation.

"I've got a casual girlfriend at home; I'd go and see her when I have some leave. Nothing serious, more of a friend with benefits, you might say. The girls here are good for a night out and a bit of a laugh when I go out with Jaimie. He is the lothario in the team. Again, nothing serious. Why boss?"

"It must be difficult for you and the others maintaining a social life when you are called away and can't say where you're going, why or when you'll be back."

"It goes with the territory boss; Special Forces is not exactly a nine to five job, is it?" Ham smiled and shook his head slowly. Ives looked out the corner of his eye at Ham and wondered what was on the old boy's mind.

"Ok," Ham seemed to recover, "The other point, I want you to tell the other lads that they have forty-eight hours from when I said, not seventy-two. Whatever happens, I want them back in two days. Don't ask, but they'll understand. Stay in town until Captain Macduff calls you. The rest of the team will be busy for a few days, but you can chill for the moment. Do a little research on Huginn H-U-G-I-N-N and Muninn M-U-N-I-N-N, you know, Google or whatever you do these days. Just F-Y-I." Ives nodded and suppressed a smile since when had the old man started to give orders in text-speak? "Right, I am going to take the beasts for their walk, and you can go and do some extreme-chilling. Tell the lads as soon as you get back to the house; they'll need all the time they've got. Off you go." Off, Ives went, and Ham watched his back as he went.

Ham stood upright and continued down to Aubrey Park to check on the swans. Whenever he walked in that area, he checked on the swans. He liked to look at them and see how the family were doing. Major also checked on them. Princess, having seen them once, ignored them; after all, they were just birds, hardly worth waking up for. Ham found their graceful swimming calming, but it was not always so.

Five And Six

He was nearly home when his phone rang, and Macduff asked to come over to the apartment. Ham agreed, and she arrived shortly afterwards. She used her keys, Janet held another set, and after announcing her presence, checked if he needed a refill. She saw his mug was nearly full, so she just made herself one. Completing this, she walked into the living room and sat down. Ham viewed her expectantly with a raise of his eyebrows.

He spoke first, "I scanned the house earlier; it's safe to talk."

"Boss, I am a bit confused. You're planning on giving Ives the full treatment; why him and not the others. John, Rob and Jaimie didn't have anything like this done to them. Even I didn't get the treatment[19]." She stopped, waited, blew on her mug and stared at Ham over her mug of scalding hot tea.

"You are not Special Forces and therefore flew under the MI6 radar. They couldn't have guessed you'd be joining the department. If you hadn't 'lumped' that guard's officer and been rescued by the general, it is possible

---

[19] See "The Boundary Walker" by Deryk Stronach

that you would not be here now." She nodded in acknowledgement. "As for the lads, they came to us by accident. Nobody, especially MI5 or MI6, could have predicted where they would end up. Steve is a slightly different case[20]; firstly, whereas the others are SBS, he is SAS, the Spooks are known to train and recruit SAS operators. I don't want Five or Six, knowing what we do. Secondly, maybe he is too good a candidate. He could be a plant."

"And what if he is? Will it be like Thompson? Does he have a little 'accident'?[21]" Ham looked horrified.

"Good grief, no! If he is tainted, we'll see if we can clean him up; put him on the right path; bring him back from the 'Dark Side'."

"And if we cannot?"

"If he's committed to MI6, then he will be RTU'd[22] with no blemish on his record."

"That's why you've been sending him on training or leave when a mission has come up. Ok, what if he comes back clean, is cleaned up, or is clean-up-able?"

---

[20] See "Never in Ones" by Deryk Stronach
[21] See "The Boundary Walker" by Deryk Stronach
[22] RTU – Returned to Unit

"Then we'll bring him fully into the fold. The general wants to get him commissioned. He sees him as a future team leader. We desperately need more teams, and I tend to agree with the old boy. Ives is academically qualified, his service record is excellent, so it's just a matter of how. I'll talk to the general about it when I see him tomorrow."

"Ok, boss, Janet says she'll come over and stay here while you're away. It'll be easier on Major and Princess. She's still pissed at you, you know. That was a dirty trick you played on her." Ham sipped his tea and hid the beginning of a faint smile behind the mug.

"Tell her I'm sorry," he said softly.

"Are you?" Macduff asked in earnest.

"Good night, captain." Finishing her tea, Macduff got up to leave after cleaning the mug, of course.

"Alison," Ham called through to the kitchen. She stuck her head in the door. "We may be having another member on the team soon, a female. You can fit her into your safe home?" Macduff nodded.

"Can do. We're going to need a bigger place to meet at this rate," Macduff said. Ham nodded.

"I'll speak to the general. By the way, what do you know of Huginn and Muninn?"

Macduff's brow creased as she concentrated and stepped fully into the room.

"Norse mythology. The two ravens reported back to Odin the goings-on in the world."

"Very good. Well done. Keep it up." Pleased with the compliment but puzzled at the question, Macduff shrugged and left.

Breakfast

Ham was the first to leave Largs. The driver picked him up and deposited him politely at Glasgow airport, where a small military passenger jet was waiting to fly him down to RAF Northolt, just outside London. He was expecting a vehicle to be waiting to drive him into the city but was surprised to find the general in the back seat.

"We'll go to my club; they serve a reasonable breakfast," the general said without looking at Ham. The general did not talk during the journey, so Ham sat quietly, occasionally looking out the window. Silences never bothered Ham; the opposite, he enjoyed them.

Arriving at the club, Gilchrist, the general's bodyguard cum driver, opened the car door. The general got out with a slight nod of thanks, and Ham followed. Ham saw Gilchrist get back in the car and drive off. Ham realised that he must have done this drop off many times and knew where to go and wait. Ham kept up with the general, greeted most civilly by the doorman who had opened the door and ushered them in. A nod from the general to the desk manager resulted in a slight stiffening of the manager's back and a respectful greeting. Ham and the general divested their coats which disappeared into the cloakroom. An attendant led them up a large, curved staircase along an opulent hallway to a fair-sized room. A small conference table surrounded by half a dozen ornate chairs: a pair of brown ageing leather armchairs bracketing a coffee table by the window stood in the room. The club had set out on the conference cum dining table two settings of gold-rimmed white bone China crockery and silver ornate cutlery.

"A full breakfast for both of us, please, Somerson. You can bring the tea to start with," the general ordered over his shoulder while he walked towards the left armchair. The general sat and waved at Ham to do the same in the other chair. The armchairs were old and worn. A particularly hard spring somewhere in the cushion, pressing uncomfortably against Ham's testicles, forced him to adjust his position.

"That chair is quite famous in the club; it is called the 'Ball-breaker'," the general guffawed. Ham smiled politely, although he was not amused. He did not come down to London to be emasculated. The general glanced, dramatically Ham thought, over his shoulder, seeing the close was clear, continued in a voice that was a little, but not much, quieter than his usual bellow, "You're probably wondering why I brought you down." Ham waited. The general looked at him, and Ham waited some more.

The tea arrived and poured. The general waited until the butler had left.

"Well?" Ham waited. The general raised an eyebrow in annoyance.

"Ok, sir, why did you bring me down here?" Ham asked and added, "I'm not moving down to London. I'm staying in Largs."

"I could force you." The general said softly. There was a hint of menace in his voice.

"I could resign," Ham replied equally softly and with a slight firmness in his tone. They stared at each other for a few minutes, neither willing to give way. Keeping his eyes on Ham, the general raised his delicate teacup and sipped his tea. Ham liked milk in his tea, so he had to break eye contact to pour the milk. Believing that he had won this minor skirmish, the general sipped his drink with a slight smirk. Ham shook his head slightly. Ham preferred his tea in a mug but knew that the 'Club' was not a place to ask for one.

Just not done, old chap. When in Rome and all that.

"So, why am I here?" Ham asked over his delicate teacup.

"I am going to resign shortly; I want you to take over the department." Ham stopped mid-sip but maintained his composure. It took a moment for Ham to gather his thoughts. He continued drinking his tea. He did not say anything, but he stared at the general.

"There is no need for you to resign. After that business in French Guiana[23], Janet slipped you that special water, your cancer is cured, and you are fit enough to go on for years yet."

"It's not a case of how long I can last; it's a matter of how long Anne can last."

"Anne?"

"My wife, Anne." Ham nodded. He never considered whether the general had a wife or not. Who the Hell would put up with him? "She is not in the best of health.

As you know, we tend to spend a lot of time away from our loved ones in this business. I want us to spend her remaining time spending time together. To do that, I need a

---

[23] See "Never in Ones" by Deryk Stronach

replacement, and you are the only obvious choice." Ham was about to reply, but the general waved him into silence. "Look what happened when the PM[24] chose that bloody Johnny Johnson as a replacement[25]. No, it has to be you." Ham thought, 'Oh Christ'.

"How on earth can I be? I don't have the authority to get things done. I'm a colonel, for God's sake. How the Hell am I supposed to get generals, admirals and Air Vice Marshalls to do what I want? They'd tell me to bugger off tout-bloody-suite[26]." At that moment, two butlers arrived with their breakfasts on large silver trays. They rose from the armchairs and took their places at the table. Having deposited the tray on the table, the butlers assisted the general and Ham with their chairs. The breakfasts served, and after a nod from the general, the butlers left silently. Of course, the meal was excellent, and they did not talk until the plates were clean.

Before he spoke, the general took out an envelope and passed it across the table. Ham looked at the envelope, the general, and back to the envelope. Without a word, he opened and read the contents. He slid the

---

[24] PM – Prime Minister
[25] See "Never in Ones" by Deryk Stronach
[26] Tout suite – very quickly

letter back into the envelope and, placing it back on the table, slid it back towards the general.

"That is attempted bribery," Ham remarked.

"No, that is a fait accompli[27] Brigadier Hamilton. You are right; you need a higher rank to deal with your job. You are a brigadier and as of today, and as of now drawing a brigadier's pay."

"I am still not moving. You know me, I cannot operate in the city, any city. If you try to force me, I shall resign. At least now, I shall retire with a brigadier's pension." The general glared at Ham. Ham smiled back as best he could. It was a smirk; Ham was not good at smiling. The general nodded as if to himself and rose from the table. Although he had not finished his toast and jam, Ham followed suit.

"Come," the general commanded. The general left, and Ham followed. If Ham were prone to showing emotions, he would have frowned, but instead, he followed the general through the club with a passive face. He knew this was not over.

---

[27] Fait accompli – An action carried out before it can be queried or reversed

Up the Chain of Command

Ham was not sure where the car was going. He did not know London, having only ever passed through it as quickly as he could. He preferred the countryside or, ideally, the seaside. Maybe he should have joined the Royal Navy, he thought.

During the twenty-minute drive, the general made a brief call on his mobile phone to say that they were on the way. Ham briefed him on what missions he had arranged for the team and why. The general seemed satisfied and told him to put it in a written report later.

They arrived, and Ham was a little bit surprised. Thinking on it a moment or two, he realised that he should not have been. It was logical. He steeled himself for what was to come. They exited the car when it drew up outside Ten Downing Street. The police constable nodded to the general outside the door, knocked once on the door, and continued his armed vigil. The door opened, and they were ushered inside.

A tall, dark-suited official, dark-haired except for greying temples adding a sophisticated style to his appearance, smiled ingratiatingly at them. Their coats were not taken; the message was simple, they would not be staying long. He did usher them deeper inside.

"This way, please general, brigadier, the Prime Minister is expecting you." This man knew that Ham was a brigadier. They entered a large yellow walled room, ornamented with a giant crystal chandelier and tall windows framed by reddish-orange curtains. There were two white-clothed armchairs and two two-seater similar coloured sofas in front of a large white fireplace. They stood in the middle of the room and looked around. Ham could see the PM's famous from many photo ops, conference table through an open door. The three men waited patiently for a couple of minutes. The Prime Minister entered, smiled and shook their hands. The PM nodded to the dark suit, who left quietly, closing the door.

General, glad to see you. You are looking better every day," he added with a conspiratorial glint in his eye. The PM was one of the very few people privy to all the reports Ham and the general submitted. Turning to Ham, he continued, "Brigadier, I've read much of your exploits. So sorry that my gaff with that idiot Johnny Johnson caused you so much trouble.[28]" A short pause. "But we are here to remedy that problem. Well, the fact that you are here means that General Maxwell has been unsuccessful in coaxing you down from the wilds of bonnie Scotland, eh?" Without waiting for a reply, he fished into his inside breast pocket and pulled out an envelope and held it out towards Ham. Ham groaned inwardly. "We need you to take over. General Maxwell cannot stay forever, and we need someone of your calibre, with your erm skills and experience to take over." Ham knew when he was being buttered up, and he hated to think was he was being baited with to move down to London and take over the department. General Maxwell coughed, and Ham snapped out of his thoughts and looked at him. The general looked at Ham and nodded to the envelope still in the hands of the PM.

Ham took the envelope, thanking the PM, and after a quick sideways look at the general, he opened it and read the contents. It seemed that he was now a major-general. He looked up sharply at the PM and the general.

"It cannot be. This is not the way it works. You don't suddenly get promotions like this.

---

[28] See "Never in Ones" by Deryk Stronach

There is a system and culture. Nobody gets promotion this quick, not even in war-time."

"I do have a certain amount of influence in military circles, you know," the PM stated with a faint smile. Now, Major General Hamilton, about you taking over the department and moving into the general's office." The PM openly smiled at Ham, knowing that he had won. The PM always won eventually; that's why he was Prime Minister. Ham looked down again at the letter of confirmation. There was a pregnant pause.

"Thank you, sir. Seeing how everyone is handing out letters, I have one to give as well." Ham reached into his inside breast pocket, and General Maxwell's eyes almost rolled to the back of his head. The PM looked puzzled. The PM accepted the letter when Ham offered it to him. He looked at the envelope, at Ham, the general and back to the letter. He opened the envelope and read the letter.

"What?" he spluttered. "You can't resign. I forbid it. Resignation refused. Dammit, I've just made you a major general, and this is how you respond." It took a moment for the PM to regain his composure. He ran his fingers through his hair in a slight nervous habit and stood, obviously in deep thought. Standing straight, he said calmly. "Gentlemen, I shall meet you at the front door shortly. And with that, he smiled his politician smile and left. Unsummoned, the dark suit entered and ushered them back the way they came, where they donned their coats and waited. The general did not speak. Ham looked at the general, but he could not catch his eye.

The Lion's Den

The drive was only just over five minutes, for it was only about a mile from Downing Street to Buckingham Palace: with police escorts, before the PM's car and after General Maxwell's car, it was even quicker, certainly smoother.

They entered the inner courtyard and alighted from their vehicles under the covered porch. The cars drove away to park, and the men were ushered in through the large double doors into the Grand Entrance. To say it was impressive would be an understatement. The Marble Hall, named after the colossal marble columns rising from the deep red carpet, lay to their right. They were taken left to the large staircase. The gilded bronze balustrade that led them up was reported to be the most expensive treasure in the building.

They were led to a large white drawing-room, which held massive crystal chandeliers, a golden piano, ornate furniture, chairs and sofas with bright yellow cushions. The room was huge; even the large fruit and flower carpet were dwarfed by its size. They were left alone. The PM who had been there many times waited patiently. The general and PM faced Ham as he faced them and the doorway awaiting the royal personage. Their faces were impassive, but their eyes glinted a hidden secret. Eventually, the general nodded to Ham and indicated that he should turn around. Puzzled, Ham did so and was confronted by the smiling figure of Her Majesty the Queen. Ham straightened immediately and stared straight ahead. The Queen is short[29] , and he found he was looking over her head. Short she may have been, but she dominated the room with her presence, a room she had entered through a concealed doorway.

They waited; you do not speak first to the Queen; rules are rules.

"Good morning, gentlemen." She walked towards and stood in front of the Prime Minister. She held out her white-gloved hand. "Prime Minister." A quick shake and a bow from the PM.

"Good morning, Your Majesty. May I present General Maxwell, who I believe you know." She walked over to the ramrod-straight general for a quick handshake.

---

[29] 1.63m or 5ft3in

"Your Majesty," he said with a stiff bow. Ham had never seen the general humbled, but even in these few words, he heard the nervousness and awe in his voice.

"How is your wife, general? I trust she is faring well?"

"Yes, Ma'am[30]. Thank you for asking; she is comfortable. May I introduce Major General Hamish Hamilton."

"Major General Hamilton, you wake up a colonel, and now you are a major general. Not a bad day, I think." Ham shook her hand and bowed.

"Yes, Your Majesty. It was not what I was expecting this morning." She laughed. She took a step back and looked at them all in turn, finally coming to rest on Ham.

"The fact you are here indicates to me that these gentlemen have been unable to convince you to take over General Maxwell's post. General Maxwell needs to retire soon for family reasons. The Prime Minister tried to find a replacement, and you know what happened[31]. We have discussed this matter,

---

[30] The first meeting of a day with her Majesty, she should be greeted with, Your Majesty, any conversation after that she is called, Ma'am.

and we all agree that you are the only choice." Ham's feelings must have shown on his face because the Queen held up her small dainty hand slightly and continued. "If you want a replacement, you will have to train that person yourself." She stiffened, and the sparkle of the smile disappeared; there was a slight firmness in the voice as she added, "to my satisfaction". She looked at him, and when the smile returned a moment later and her posture relaxed slightly, he knew that he was being allowed to speak.

"Ma'am, I have always operated in the field; I am not a desk-bound warrior. No offence meant to the general. No matter how important the work is, I cannot take a post in London. I need the countryside or the sea; I cannot survive in a city. I could not serve you well." The Queen's expression did not waver. She turned to General Maxwell.

"You have not told him yet?"

"No, Ma'am, as we agreed, it should come from you." She nodded and turned back to Ham.

---

[31] See "Never in Ones" by Deryk Stronach

"Major General Hamilton, I understand that you insist on staying in Largs, at least basing yourself there?" Ham nodded.

"Yes, Ma'am, I'm from that area." As if that made the slightest difference to Her Majesty the Queen. "I grew up on the Isle of Cumbrae and wish to retire in that area. The queen nodded.

"I can understand that I went to Largs a long time ago," a short pause. "1958 with my late husband. He launched a small boat that we had donated to the sailing school, a Windlass, I believe, from Cairnie Quay. We travelled down by Royal Train, the place was covered in bunting, and there was such a lovely crowd. The weather was kind to us that day. My cousin Lord Louis Mountbatten commandeered a couple of hotels there during the war and used them with all the senior allied officers to plan the D-Day landings. My father, King George, flew up there in an RAF Catalina flying boat accompanied by Prime Minister Churchill. He said that nobody paid him any attention because they all thought he was Lord Mountbatten," she smiled," they were very similar in appearance. My mother went up there in 1979. The Princess Royal has been there a few times, she loves sailing in that area, she was there to open of the pier in 2009 after its reconstruction, and for the opening of the new RNLI Boathouse on the Largs Promenade in 1998, near the hotels where Lord Mountbatten planned D-Day. She went across to Millport. We've all thought it is a lovely area; I can understand that you want to stay in that area, but is it practical? Wouldn't a Royal Navy, Royal Air Force or army base be more convenient?" Ham was surprised at the depth of the Queen's background and knowledge of the area.

"Ma'am, for the same reasons that Lord Mountbatten chose Largs as the place to plan D-Day, it is still a good choice for the department, it is fairly secluded, but accessible, not only to major roads but airports and the sea. There are military bases nearby that we can use if we need. If we were stationed on a base, we would attract attention from the wrong people." Ham did not elaborate on who the wrong people might be. There were a lot of military, civil service and intelligence people that would love to find out what MIC was up to, hence the problem with Ives.

"I understand, and what are you doing about Corporal Ives? How will you learn if he is suitable for the department?" Ham did not think that the Queen would be so informed about the running of MIC. He was momentarily stunned.

"I am sending him to Shaman Drygeese; she will know if he is tainted. I hope he is not, as I believe he will make a good team leader in the future."

"Yes, keep me up to date on that, please." She paused momentarily, then continued, "General Maxwell has been working on a building in Largs. From the plans that I have seen, it should meet the immediate needs of your team." Ham remembered the large red sandstone building with the high surround fencing on the Largs seafront that was being rebuilt or modified. "General Maxwell will explain all this to you fully later. We are not expecting you to move from Largs, MIC is moving to Largs, and you will be placed in charge of it when General Maxwell retires." Ham was speechless. The Queen turned and walked over to a chest of drawers. She opened a drawer and took out an envelope. Returning to stand in front of Ham, she held out the envelope. Ham took it thinking it was the blueprints or deeds or whatever from the site. He took the envelope and thanked her.

"I think you are supposed to open it," said the PM quietly. Ham did so. Lieutenant general![32] Holy Shit! He looked up at the Queen, who smiled back at him warmly.

"I have some influence with the military," she said with a disarming smile. "We knew you would not accept leaving your beloved Largs. The general probably knows you better than you know yourself. He has been arranging the construction or reconstruction of your new headquarters for over a year. The Prime Minister knows that you will need to hold sufficient rank to get the other senior officers to listen to you, but it will be up to you to persuade them to your will. Ham glanced at the PM, who did his best and failed at hiding a smirk. It was an, I got you, smirk. Ham knew he had been played all along. "You cannot be a lieutenant general," the Queen continued, without holding the rank of a brigadier and a major general; procedures must be followed. You will visit London as ordered, where the general will train you as you will, in turn, later, train your successor or successors in the future."

---

[32] A major is higher than a lieutenant, as the rank of major general used to be 'sergeant major general', hence lieutenant general is higher than major general.

"Ma'am, how can I be any general? I know nothing of how to be a lieutenant general."

"Lieutenant General Hamilton, you will never lead a Corps or an army into battle, but you will run your department and look after my creatures, yes, my creatures. All the people and creatures in my Kingdom are under my protection, and you are the man who is going to do the protecting."

"Yes, Ma'am."

"I have read all your reports and adventures. It has been a pleasure meeting you. I'm sure we shall meet again. Congratulations. Keep up the good work." And with a slight nod, she left; the audience was over.

The Queen left through the same concealed door, back to her apartments, and the three men were escorted down the stairs to their waiting vehicles.

"I was a bit worried that you might refuse," laughed the general.

Without turning his head, Ham replied, "Nobody refuses the Queen. That's treason." General Maxwell and the PM looked at Ham, not knowing if he was serious.

The Lieutenant General Returns

Ham politely refused an offer to remain in London for the night, partly because he wanted to be home in Largs and partially because he did not wish to detain the general away from his wife.

On the journey back to RAF Northolt, they again discussed what the team was up to, how Ham would deal with his new base of operations when it was complete and especially about how they were going to deal with the information that the ravens Huginn and Muninn had delivered. They decided that the general would contact his counterpart in Norway and formulate a plan. The message that Ham had received from the birds meant that Elves expected Ham's team to act upon the information, but it was in Norway and the co-operation of the Norwegians that was paramount. As the general so succinctly put it, "One does not simple shit in one's neighbour's garden, without their permission". The general thought this funny and guffawed for a few minutes. Ham waited patiently until the general had finished laughing at his humour; before getting back to the matters in hand. Reports had been received of brutal murders in the Scottish Highlands. The

Scottish Police had been told to suppress the information on the grounds of national security and public interest. The order had been passed over at the highest level, with dire consequences promised for any breach. The general expected Ham's team to deal with the matter quickly. The sooner it was dealt with, the less chance of a leak. A leak, of course, there would be, but the general would manage its content.

As he left the car at the bottom of the aircraft stairs, the general told Ham to wait. Ham looked around and saw a woman escorted by an Air Movements Operator walk out from the Air Movement Terminal walk towards them. She was blond, her hair tied back in a simple ponytail, about 175cms high, slim built with a quite extraordinary good figure. Ham was lousy at guessing people's ages, especially women, so he could only assume her to be between mid-forties to early fifties. He narrowed the gap to mid-forties to late forties as she drew closer. Her pale blue eyes sparkled as she walked towards the general. She stopped in front of Maxwell and handed him a black briefcase that had seen better days.

The general nodded thanks and, in turn, handed the briefcase to Ham. Without turning around, the general stated, "Ms Miller, please meet Lieutenant General Hamilton, Hamilton, Ms Lucinda Miller. Do you have transport, Lucinda?"

"Yes, Sir."

"Good, then off you go, and I'll see you tomorrow in the office." Lucinda Miller smiled at the general, then Ham and turned and left.

"She lives in Ruislip, just down the road. Good girl. She will be a great asset to you. The briefcase contains what you think it does. Read that lot; go along there when you can. If you need any changes, let me know as soon as possible. Ham weighed the briefcase in his hand. It was heavy. That was an awful lot of documents for blueprints and documents relating to the new construction. Ham wished he had been involved in the process earlier as he was sure there would be changes and amendments he would have wanted to make.

Ham shook the general's hand, turned and made towards the steps. Unlike the Americans, the British military does not salute unless they are in uniform and wearing a uniform hat. Ham glanced around out of habit. He saw Ms Miller disappear into the building, an RAF Policeman hovering around in the background, just in case. The RAF DAMO[33] stood to the left, and three airmen 'Movers'[34] stood to attention to the right of the stairs. Trying not to look as awkward as he felt, he shook the DAMO's hand and nodded to the airmen before he made his way up the steps. The RAF Air Steward showed him to his seat and made him safe and comfortable. Once in the air, Ham was asked if he wanted refreshments; he agreed to a tea and some small delicate triangles of sandwiches, egg and the slimmest slivers of cucumber and ham and cheese. Ham guessed they had recently come out of a fridge as they were cool to the point of cold., but that didn't matter as the tea was scolding hot. Waiting until the steward had retired back to his curtained-off kitchenette. Ham took the files out of the briefcase.

Sipping his tea and taking care not to knock the cup over, Ham opened and studied the files and plans. Closing everything up and replacing them into the briefcase, he asked for another cup; it wasn't any good, but he needed tea to think. He sat back with the briefcase on the seat next to him and the cup in his hand. Surprisingly, he decided that he

---

[33] DAMO – Duty Air Movements Officer
[34] Movers – Air Movements Operators or Controllers.

would have made relatively few changes. The old boy had made an excellent job of it, much better than Ham would have given him credit.

Ham wondered how he was to fill the general's shoes.

When he arrived home, he found that Janet had forgiven him and was eager to learn what had happened. When he told her that he was now a lieutenant general, she did not seem impressed, which puzzled Ham for a moment until he realised that she did not have a military background and one military rank was the same as the rest. Inwardly, and maybe a bit self-consciously, Ham was waiting to tell Macduff and the lads, they would understand.

Meanwhile, Ham had a dog to take for a walk and a cat to carry. Janet accepted his invitation to join them. A pleasant early evening's walk on the Promenade and a chance for Ham to plan his next moves.

The Warriors Return

Late the next day, Rob, much to his chagrin, was the first to arrive back with his metaphorical tail between his legs. He reported back, but Ham could see that he had failed in his mission and was not a happy bunny. Ham told him that he would debrief him the next day when the others returned, Ham would let him know when. In the meantime, he was to go back to the safe house, get cleaned up and chill. He could hunker down with a few drinks, but Ham 'recommended'[35] that he stay in the house and recover until the others returned. Secretly, Ham did not want Rob going out after his failure and saying something he should not. Rob was an experienced Special Forces Operative who had carried out many missions and Black Ops[36], but Ham wanted to be on the safe side. It was because Rob was so good at his job and was not used to failure that Ham wanted him to have time to unwind. Ham was also sure that he would not be the only one to fail.

---

[35] For recommended, read ordered
[36] Black Ops – Those missions deemed too secret for a written record to be kept.

Jaimie was next; he was not quite so depressed, as he had seen the target but had been grabbed before he could take a photo. Ham told him it was a nice try, but no picture, no banana. In other words, the operation was a success, but the patient died. His mission was to photograph the target and bring it back. Jaimie's excitement gave way to depression. Ham felt sorry for him, but rules were rules. Ham reminded him not to talk about the mission with anyone and go back to the safe house and chill like Rob.

The last to arrive back was John. He reported back more than a little dishevelled, smelling to high heavens, so much so that Major and Princess left the room. He was straight-faced serious as he stood in front of Ham. They stared at each other for a few moments.

"So, you have the photos then," Ham stated. John opened his jacket and pulled out a small GoPro digital camera. Ham raised his eyebrows at the sight of it.

"This is not the one you were issued with?" queried Ham.

"After I took the photos with both cameras, I knew they were on to me, they were good, so I deliberately dropped the issued camera accidental like, and made off with the GoPro that I guessed they didn't know I had. I assumed their game was to stop me bringing the photos back; mine was to make them believe that they had succeeded." Ham took the camera and, powering it on, viewed the photos. Ham nodded.

"Well done, John, well done. Very few manage first time, if at all. I'll keep this for a while. I hope you don't have any photos you want on this because they will be securely wiped. I must ask, did you make any copies?" Paterson shook his head firmly.

"No sir,"

"I had to ask. I trust you, John." Ham paused. "Now comes the hard bit. You cannot talk to the other two about what you photographed. Jaimie saw what you saw but failed to capture them on film. On this mission, that is a failure. In the future, when we have time, they can try again. If they succeed, you can discuss the mission with them in a safe environment, not until. I'll tell you when. Understand?"

"Yessir."

"I think it would be a good idea if you went and cleaned up; you do stink quite a bit, you know. I'll debrief you tomorrow when you smell better."

"Yessir. One question though, boss, if I may, who were those men?" Ham knew who he meant.

"They're called the Queen's Ghillies[37]. They are all selected veterans whose sole purpose is to protect what's on the island, one of the biggest secrets in the Kingdom. Think of them as the Special Forces of the Chelsea Pensioners[38]." Ham still had not got the habit of chuckling or laughing out loud, but he nearly did. Nothing is as funny as one's own jokes. "I'll tell you more about it all tomorrow, John. You look like you need a rest. Tell Rob I'll see him here tomorrow at ten hundred hours." Ham looked at Paterson and wondered whether to tell him about his promotion to lieutenant general but decided to tell Macduff first as she was his second in command. It would not do for her to find out from one of the men. Although he had not

[37] Ghillies – Scots. Expert fishing and hunting guides. The camouflage suit worn by military snipers worldwide is called a Ghillie suit after a design the ghillies perfected hunting deer in the wilds of Scotland.
[38] Chelsea Pensioners – Residents of the Royal Hospital Chelsea, about 300 strong of army veterans who are cared for after service to the crown. They are normally seen in black trousers, red coats and black tricorn hats.

sought the promotion, deep inside, he was proud that it had been given to him; no, it had not been given; it had been earned. Understanding that the meeting was over, Paterson smiled, nodded and left.

Ham hoped that everything was going well with Ives. Macduff would only be gone a couple of days. Ives a bit longer, months maybe. Ham trusted the Shaman to do what was right. She seemed to know what was needed and when. He did not know how that was going to go. Ham's gift allowed him to see the creatures and a person's life force. He could usually see how long a person had to live if he took off his pouch, but he was not gifted with seeing the future. Some Boundary Walkers could. In a way, Ham was glad of that small mercy. Second Sight could be a burden as well as a gift. He knew Ives had the Second Sight, but he did not yet know what form it took. He would find out when the time was right.

Ham wished his dad was around to see him get his promotion. When Ham did not wear the pouch, he sometimes received visits from the dead; that was why he wore it when off duty. He had to admit that he mostly wore it to keep his two late wives away; no man wants to be told twenty-four-seven what he should be doing and how. That nearly drove him insane. Individually and when they were alive, they were fine, but it was too much when they teamed up on him from the afterlife. Strangely enough, Ham never received visits from his parents after their passing. Ham did not understand what went on on the other side of the veil. He knew he would find out soon enough, even though Janet had slipped him and General Maxwell a small amount of the Water of Life.

What was he supposed to do when he passed over, an Obi Wan Kenobi on Macduff, "Feel the Force Alison"?

Ham chuckled to himself and took the beasts for a walk. Major followed, occasionally wandering onto the grass for a sniff and pee. If Major looked as if he was about to squat, Ham would dig into his pocket for a small bio-degradable bag. Is this the job for a lieutenant general, a pooper-scooper?

Of Missile Ranges and Biological Testing Sites

"How did they get onto me so quickly?" Rob asked. Ham had electronically searched the whole apartment that morning before Rob had arrived, so he knew it was safe to talk about the mission. Ham sat comfortably in his dark brown beaten up old leather club armchair; Rob sat nearby on the sofa, puzzled, confused and eager to learn where he went wrong. He had not talked to the other two about the mission, and they as ordered had not talked about it to him. Rob could take failure, he had been on missions that had gone tits-up[39], but that did not mean that he had to like it. Ham looked at the first of the three files marked, 'Above Top Secret', even though he had memorised the contents as soon as the courier had delivered the files.

"You HAHO'd[40] in at night. Normally a good choice, especially as you were aiming at a target on the edges of the Atlantic Ocean. But remember, this island is out of bounds to civilians because it lies under the missile

---

[39] Tits-up – Military slang, failed
[40] HAHO – A military parachuting technique, High Altitude High Opening. Exit aeroplane, deploy parachute and guid yourself to the target, which could be many kilometres away

testing range, a forbidden area. The three services are firing missiles over it all the time—a good excuse to keep the general public and any unwanted nosey types out of the way. Various radar systems monitor the missile tests and, of course, keep people safely out of the way. Most radars would not have picked you up, but these are better than most. We didn't tell them that you were coming; it was as much a test for them as for you. If they hadn't spotted you, there would have been serious questions asked."

"You said not to go in armed or offer any serious resistance; what if I had?" Ham looked Rob straight in the eye.

"You and I would probably not be talking now." Rob blinked.

"OK, boss. I failed. What happens now? Do I get RTU'd[41] or something?"

"No, you go away and plan how to do it next time. Don't put too much effort into that just now; we have other missions to worry about. You'll have another crack at it. Most do not get it the first time. When we have time, I'll send you in again."

"Did you?"

---

[41] RTU – Returned to Unit

"Did I what?"

"Did you manage the mission the first time?" They looked at each other for a few minutes, both faces devoid of expression.

"That questions a bit impertinent to ask your boss, isn't it?" Rob started to apologise, but Ham held up his hand and smiled as best he could. "Go back to the safe house and tell Jaimie to report soonest, please." Rob stood up and started towards the door.

"Back in the day when cameras were bulky black and white contraptions that needed flash for night shots, I was supposed to bring back a photo. I was young and cocky, so I brought a young one back and presented it to my team leader, Janet's late husband, Jack Drummond. It caused a bit of a stink and nearly got me kicked out of the department. Luckily General Jensen, General Maxwell's predecessor had a sense of humour, so I got away with it, but he made me do the mission again, making it harder by telling the ghillies when I was due to arrive."

"Thanks, boss," Rob said and left. Ham got up and made a mug of tea.

The Queen's Secret

Ham had finished his drink by the time Jaimie arrived. Ham sat in his armchair and scanned the second file on his lap. It seemed that both the operators had listened to Ham's warning about the Great White Sharks, as he too opted to parachute onto the island, but instead of HAHOing like Rob, he selected HALOing.[42] He looked up at Jaimie, who was nursing a mug of steaming tea in both his hands.

"Right, I've scanned the apartment earlier, so we can talk freely, but keep your voice down as we can't take any chances with this."

"Boss, who grabbed me? I thought I was good at the stealth stuff, but those guys came out of nowhere."

"They're called the Queen's Ghillies. They are all ex-Special Forces, top of the range snipers or similar. I believe the recruitment criteria is rather thorough."

---

[42] HALO – a military parachuting technique, High Altitude Low Opening. Exiting the aircraft but delaying the deployment of the parachute until the last moment. HALOing also allows for some lateral transfer, but not as much as HAHOing, but it does allow for a faster, less easy to spot even on radar descent.

"Sir, I don't understand. What's the big secret? What I saw doesn't seem that important. At least not different from the Kelpies, Selkies, Dragons and Yetis we've all seen. I don't get it." Ham got up and walked over to his bureau, opened a drawer and took out his passport. He handed it to Jaimie.

"What animals do you see?" he asked.

"A lion and a Unicorn," Jaimie replied, handing the passport back.

"The lion represents England and the Unicorn Scotland, right?" Jaimie nodded; he guessed so; he had never thought about it before. "Seen many lions in England recently, apart from zoos or safari parks?" Jaimie looked confused as he was not sure where this was going.

"It is said that when English explorers travelled the world colonising anything they put their foot on in the name of the Crown, they came across the lion, the King of the Jungle, and took this symbol of bravery, nobility, royalty, strength, stateliness and courage to represent England. Many countries took the lion symbol and incorporated it into their national crest, Norway, Denmark, Belgium, Spain. It is thought that the lions they all took as their symbols were the Barbary Lions of North Africa. North Africa was certainly within travelling distance for all these nations." Jaimie still looked puzzled. "The other animal is the mythical Unicorn, right." Jaimie nodded.

"Have you heard the saying that when the last of the apes leave Gibraltar, it will be lost to the British Crown?" Jaimie nodded. Ham continued, "What you may not know is that in 1944, in the middle of the Second World War, the ape numbers were decreasing. Churchill ordered that Macaque apes, or old-world monkeys as they are technically called, be smuggled from Morocco to Gibraltar to sustain their numbers on the Rock. They did this to stop the Spanish or the Germans using the legend to lower morale amongst the Gibraltarians, or use the lack of apes to increase the pressure on the British by the Spanish who wanted their rock back." Ham paused.

"As you said, the other animal on my passport was the Unicorn. You saw Unicorns on the island. The lion is English, the Scottish. There is a not so well known legend that when the last Unicorn leaves Scotland, the United Kingdom as a Crown nation will cease to exist. Now, everybody believes that

Unicorns are only mythological creatures, so the legend hardly gets a mention. But what would happen if it became known that they existed. All Hell would break loose. Unicorns are worth their weight in diamonds. Every zoo would want one, every private collector; every hunter would want one on their wall, billionaires would pay a fortune to give one to their precious little Princess daughters. But more important, certain countries would want to wipe out their numbers to legitimise the claim that the United Kingdom should be broken up. To break up the UK in such a manner would cause havoc to our nation. I'm not a politician, and I'm not interested in politics, but I am a Royalist. Yes, some of the royal family can be absolute idiots, but a sudden cataclysmic destruction of the Crown would cause chaos. The Queen is one of the few who know about the Unicorns, and she wants them looked after. To look after them, they must remain a secret. Your mission was a test for you, but it was also a test for the guards and the security systems in place. Your plane was monitored, your descent was monitored and when you HALO'd, the sound of your parachute cracking open told the ghillies exactly where you were or near enough. The rules of the test are clear. I'm sorry, but you failed, you did not bring a photograph back. But don't worry, when things are quieter, you can have another go. Those are the rules set out by Her Majesty, and her father before her and his father, going back I don't know how far, back to the beginning of our department. I don't know what they had to do in the old days before cameras, draw a sketch, paint a picture, cut a piece off one of their tails. Anyway, every operator in the department must pass this test at some point. Until you do, you cannot talk about it to anyone but me."

"But surely the Russians or whoever, with all their super-duper technology, would have taken pictures of the island. They could just turn up in a submarine and either kill or take the lot away?"

"The Russians also have their secrets that they know, we know. Maybe they'll tell you about them when you work with them in the future. Our department is different from any other; we work closely, well, pretty closely, with other countries' cryptid departments. The general decides how close and when."

"Everyone else believes that the island is lethal because of Anthrax tests carried out last century. Nobody wants to go near it. That island is protected better than you know.

There are more than Unicorns on that island." There was a pause as that sank in.

"You sent us unarmed to that island. You're implying that there were other dangerous creatures on the island; you put all our lives at risk. I don't mind risking my life, boss, but for a test…" Jaimie was not upset, but Ham could see that he was about to get that way quickly. Ham held up his hand.

"The ghillies monitor the creatures on the island. They know what is where and what they are doing. If they saw one of the other creatures stalking you, they would have intervened because you were unarmed."

"Glad to hear that. I hope they are as good at their job as you seem to think." The corner of Jaimie's mouth twisted into an ironic smile.

"They caught you, didn't they?" came the simple reply. Jaimie chose to ignore the question. It was rhetorical, he decided.

"What happened before the rumours of anthrax, before the missiles, before the ghillies? Anybody could have sailed to that island. How come there are no rumours or tales of the Unicorns?" Jaimie asked.

"The Unicorns were not always living on that island; the department moved them there when the mainland forests became too small, warnings went out about the Anthrax tests. Oh, yes, there are some Scottish islands that nobody is allowed near due to Anthrax tests, but not that one. Before that, they were looked after in certain Scottish forests by locals; a certain clan took it upon themselves to guard the secret literally with their lives. The legend of the Unicorns and the Crown is forgotten because the Unicorns have been so well protected. Anyway, that's a story for another day. We will talk no more about it today. When you've finished your tea, go back to the safe house and send John to me please." Ham looked at the wall clock and out the window at the sky. "Second thoughts, tell him to meet me at the boating pond. I think Major and I need to stretch our legs. We might even encourage Princess to exercise a little."

"Jaimie, another mission is on the offing when Captain Macduff comes back. If you are going to unwind with Rob, do it tonight. You'll need your wits about you. I would not put your lives in danger without telling you first." Jaimie stood up.

"Thanks, boss," he said with a wry smile. "I think."

Death Sentence in the Bureau

Ham replaced the three files into the safe concealed in the bureau. That done, he spun the lock several times, seven to be precise, and pushed a hidden switch elsewhere in the bureau. He hoped that no one would tamper with the safe as it would now involve getting a 'Clean-up' team and the official decorators in to tidy up the mess, not to mention some awkward explanations to the local police. Also, Ham did not want to sit on his sofa watching TV with bits of bodies hanging from the ceiling.

Ham knew that Maddox might try, or at least send his goons in to try, but Ham thought that it was a step too far even for Maddox. If Maddox got hold of those files, Ham knew he would have to deal with him severely, permanently, with extreme prejudice, or whatever it was called these days.

Ham considered the taking of life a serious matter, but in Maddox's case... Why was Maddox snooping around Largs? What was he up to? Maybe, Ham should have dealt with him permanently when he had the chance in Canada. When he wondered about Maddox, he asked himself if his decision had been weak or morally correct. To let Maddox walk away with his memory wiped of the Canadian incident seemed right at the time, but after discussions with the more blood-thirsty general, Ham was not so sure. Maybe he should have asked the Shaman to wipe ex-Colonel Maddox's mind about cryptids entirely, permanently. Maddox may have been his counterpart in the American cryptid team, but they were miles apart morally. Ham saw the cryptids as living creatures; Maddox saw them as dollar signs.

Ham knew that Maddox's boss had not trusted him completely during his tenure as the American team leader, but he never learned if Maddox was a Boundary Walker; his life force signature was clouded and confusing. Was he simply a Special forces Officer who had somehow wrangled his position, or was he gifted? To be honest, the least Ham had to know about or do with Maddox, the happier he was. Commander Jack Slaughter, the present team leader, was a different kettle of fish, sharing many of Ham's values, albeit with an American lean. Ham considered Slaughter a safe bet, whereas he considered Maddox an out and out loser.

Ham got his jacket, rucksack, beasts, weapon, a Browning 9mm High Power pistol from its concealed gun safe and left the flat to meet Warrant Officer John Paterson. He hoped his bureau would still be in one piece when he got back. Ham liked a quiet life.

Déjà Vu

Ham's quiet chat with ex-Colonel Maddox did not start well; it nearly got Maddox a hole in the head.

Ham walked along the promenade towards Aubrey Park. Noticing that there were quite a few groups of people looking at the swans, sitting casually on the benches enjoying the sunshine and the light sea breeze, picnicking on the grass, he decided to stop between the RNLI Boathouse and the park. It was quieter, and the promenade was wider. Yes, people were wandering past, but they were just dog walkers and tourists out for a walk.

Ham waited, leaning on the railings and watching a father show his kids how to skim stones over the water. Major sat, then lay down beside him. Even before Major reacted, Ham's senses told him to turn quickly; as he did, he reached inside his pocket for his gun and clicked off the safety. With his hand firmly on the grip, he faced Maddox. Major stood silently beside him, braced.

"Now it is my turn, Lieutenant General Hamilton. Look on your chest, and you will see a red dot, which of course, is from a laser sight attached to a sniper's rifle. The roles are reversed from the last time we met like this, are they not." Maddox snickered. For a grown man to snicker like a child did not improve Ham's view of the fellow. Ham looked up and looked Maddox in his beady cunning eyes.

"Take your hands out of your pockets, lieutenant general, slowly, if you don't mind. Very slowly." A grin grew on Maddox's face. When Ham did not move, Maddox's grin hardened. "Now," he hissed.

"No, I don't think so," Ham replied casually. For a fleeting moment, an expression of uncertainty passed over Maddox's eyes. "We both know you are not going to shoot. If you do, true, I shall be dead, but this hair-trigger will send a nine-millimetre bullet into your head, your forehead, to be exact, just above your nose. I'm quite a good shot, you know, even from this position. Secondly, Major here would take my demise unkindly and place those titanium teeth around your neck; you came here not to kill me but to get information. I can't give you that information if I am dead, can I? Thirdly, I know when I will die, and it's not today. You know some of the powers that I have. Maybe it is a good time to mention that your life force, on the other hand, is fragile. What was it we used to say in the old days, "Don't buy any LPs or big books; it would be a waste of money?" What would they say now, 'Don't download any albums?'" Maddox looked uncomfortable. This encounter was not going the way he planned. Ham's mobile phone rang. He released the weapon, slowly reached into his trouser pocket, and took the phone out. Ignoring Maddox, he looked at the screen and after pressing to accept the call, he placed it against his ear.

"Yes?" The caller spoke; Ham listened quietly. Maddox was dumbfounded. He looked like he did not know what to do. His expression hardened, and he looked like he was about to speak. Ham grunted into the phone. At the same time, Ham tapped his chest, now devoid of any red laser dot. He then pointed to Maddox's chest. Maddox looked at him uncomprehendingly for a moment. He then looked at his chest; there was nothing. Ham twirled his finger to indicate that Maddox should turn around. He did so slowly and looked down at his chest. Ham saw him stiffen. Ham replaced the mobile phone into his pocket.

"Maddox," Ham called firmly but softly. Maddox turned to face him. "What do you want?" If looks could kill, Ham would have been in a rather dangerous place. Controlling his anger, Maddox spoke.

"What happened in Canada? What did you do to me? I want to know what happened?"

"I'll trade you." Maddox looked confused.

"For what?" he hissed.

"How do you know that I am a lieutenant general?"

"I was told." Ham responded by rolling his eyes in a show of exasperation.

"Yes, I know that, but I want to know by whom. Who is the mole who told you? I want their name." Ham could see that Maddox was thinking, and knowing Maddox, he knew he would lie. "You have a choice; you can tell me the truth, and I will tell you what you want to know, or you can lie, and I will order my men to kill you on sight. I wouldn't give you twenty-four hours. We already knew you were here, but I must admit, I didn't think you would be so blatant as to approach me directly. Well? As a friend of mine so bluntly put it, 'Shit or get off the pot.'" Maddox was hesitant. Ham raised an eyebrow to indicate that he did not have all day to wait. Ham replaced his hands in his pockets, a sign that the meeting was over. He began to turn.

"Millerston!" Maddox called out.

"Who is Millerston?" Ham asked, turning to face Maddox.

"He's your Prime Minister's Personal Assistant." Ham looked surprised that Maddox's reach was so high.

"Describe him," Ham demanded.

"Malcolm Millerston, about six-foot, black hair greying at the temples, long fingers like a piano player, probably a closet faggot, walks like he has a broomstick shoved up his ass." Ham knew who Millerston was, the dark suit that had taken them into the PM.

"Canada?" queried Maddox hopefully. He did not give a damn about Millerston; he just looked after himself. Another Millerston could be bought.

"You went up to Canada looking for the Bigfoot Sanctuary. You took two large teams thinking numbers would be enough. We took care of your first team. I don't know if they were bait, but they were rank amateurs. If you have to recruit that level of contractors now, you are in serious trouble. You came in with your second team, you did not find the sanctuary, but you were close enough for the Bigfoot.... Is that Bigfoots or Bigfeet? I never know which, to capture you and your second team. Rather than kill you directly, their Shaman wiped your memory of the whole incident in Canada and released you. I think you might like to know that I was given a choice to kill you, cut your head clean off, but their chief persuaded me not to. It was a close call. I also have to admit that if that choice ever comes up again, I cannot say which way it would go."

"How did the Shaman wipe my mind? What did the Shaman do?" Ham shook his head. Maddox suffered from selective hearing. He came to find out what happened to his memory, which was all he was interested in.

"I honestly don't know. Herbs? Magic? I honestly don't know. But I do know something; I strongly advise you to stay out of Canada; they might not be so lenient next time. You could lose your head, literally."

"Where is this Shaman?" Maddox asked.

"You are not listening, are you? If you go near them, you will lose your head, I mean it. They will rip your head clean off. Drop it, man!" Ham saw in his eyes that he would not. Ham was past caring.

Ham looked over his shoulder. John approached, carrying a large hard plastic rifle case.

"I found someone playing with this toy, so I took it away from him. What do you want me to do with it?"

"Keep it for now. Clean it store it. It was illegal in this country, I'm sure. The general's assistant will tell you what to do with it." As Ham spoke, he ignored Maddox. Turning to Maddox, he said, "I think our business is complete here, don't you?" Maddox's shoulders slumped. He turned to leave.

"Don't you want to know what happened to your man?" Maddox turned and looked at Paterson, but Maddox seemed not to care.

"He'll wake up with a headache, minus this rifle, his pistol, his knife, his knuckle duster and baton. A right little urban warrior that one." Paterson looked down and tapped his jacket pockets as he spoke. Maddox had already left.

"Did I ruin his party?" Paterson asked innocently.

"Just a little," Ham replied. "Do they use laser sighting for sniper shooting?" Paterson shook his head slowly with a sad look on his face.

"Only amateurs," he replied. "To work out distance maybe, lasers don't take into account a bullet trajectory. Lasers are ok for CQB stuff in the dark, but sniper… Nah." Paterson shook his head. "As I said, amateurs. He must be struggling for staff." Ham nodded.

"Major's had his walk for now. We'll take a quick walk around the park to give Maddox time to slither off. You peel off and dump the ordinance back in the safe house armoury and make your way back to my place. I'll scan the place so that we can talk freely and put the kettle on." They walked silently. On the way back, the lieutenant general pooper scooper did his duty to the community.

After scanning the flat, Ham did his duty to the nation and called the general about the PM's treacherous PA. After that, what happened to him was up to the general, but the poor fellow was in for a lousy time judging by past history.

Six's Games

Paterson took longer than expected to arrive at the flat. Ham had already scanned the flat for audio and visual bugs. Nothing had been disturbed. The place was clean. Ham had finished his second mug of tea when Paterson arrived at the front door. Ham didn't say anything, just raised an eyebrow when Paterson walked in with his finger to his lips.

Leaning into Ham's ear, Paterson spoke very softly, "Have you scanned the place." Ham looked at him and nodded. "We need to do it again, thoroughly. I'll explain later." They found two of them. Ham could kick himself, but he was damned sure that they were not there yesterday. He should have checked just as thoroughly today as yesterday. These devices were the type only activated when someone spoke or made similar sounds; otherwise, they lay dormant and harder to detect. They went from room to room, talking banalities, scanning thoroughly, searching until they were satisfied.

Ham had the decision to either operate knowing the bugs were there and feed the listener false information or destroy them.

Ham judged the latter, and the smashed pieces went into the bin.

"Well done; what brought that inspired search on?" Ham asked.

"An itch. After I left you to walk back to the house, I got an itch between my shoulder blades; I wandered about enjoying the view until I spotted my tail or tails. I went into Tesco's and wandered around the store, looking kind of disinterestedly. There I called Rob and Jaimie. They came and tailed the tails. There were six of them altogether, cycling through permutations so that I hopefully would not spot one individual following me. I bought a train ticket to Glasgow and waited innocently for the next train to leave. They followed suit. I boarded, they boarded. As the train pulled away, I jumped off; the lads stopped anyone else doing the same. They might have been a bit heavy-handed. We checked for tails afterwards and didn't find any. However, you have a few unlikely tourists, dog-walkers and lovers in cars outside. I left Rob and Jaimie to watch them and came up. They knew about me, I guess because we met, but they didn't know about the other two, so I guess the safe house is safe for the moment. Ham walked over to his bureau and, after deactivating the explosives, checked the contents of his safe. The various safeguards and tell-tales told him that nobody had been in the safe—that and the fact that the upstairs neighbour was not peering through a hole in the floor.

"Phone the lads and tell them to bring the easiest one they can grab up here. Tell them to use force and let the others see it, but I only want one up here. Paterson nodded and rang Rob. Meanwhile, Ham set up a kitchen chair next to the kitchen table. Behind the left front leg, he duct-taped several chopping boards and metal trays to the chair leg. Standing back, he admired his handy work and searched around in his tool kit. He placed the remaining Duct Tape, plyers, screwdrivers, awls and large kitchen knives on the kitchen table. Hearing the doorbell, Paterson let in Rob, Jaimie and their new friend. The new friend, a young man in his mid to late twenties and in need of a haircut and a good shave, did not seem happy. He sported a reddening of the side of his face and neck. As Paterson led the way into the kitchen, he could not help but notice the apparent shape of a pistol with a cylinder nearby, probably a suppressor or, as it is commonly called in Hollywood, a silencer, lying nearby on the table under a kitchen towel beside the other objects. If he was surprised, he did not show it.

"Sit him down and tape his mouth," Ham ordered in a stern, commanding tone. "Tape his hands behind his back for now. I'll start with his feet. If I need to work on his hands, I'll work up to them." The man tried to struggle, but a generous slap by Paterson changed his mind. The prisoner shook his head until Rob held it firmly, facing straight ahead at the expressionless Ham. Ham shook his head slowly while still staring at the young man.

"Do not struggle as that would only cause you more pain," he said calmly to the young man. Ham was tempted to use a good Teutonic James Bond evil villain voice for a brief second but decided against the drama.

"You did remove any wires, mikes etc.?" Paterson nodded indignantly. Ham controlled the urge to smile. "You," looking at Jaimie, Ham did not want to use names, "go the front door. Take him with you," pointing at the dog, "and stop anyone trying to damage my door, use what force is necessary, that door cost me a lot. You go to the living room and check what our friends outside are doing. You,"

Paterson was the only one left in the room apart from Ham and the curious cat, "stay with our playmate here. I'll be back to deal with him shortly. Try not to hurt him yet; I'll say when and how." Ham left the room. First, he went to Jaimie and spoke to him quietly and then to Rob. Leaving them, Ham walked into the bedroom and, closing the doors, sat on the bed and rang the general. During a short, softly spoken conversation, Ham told him about Maddox's visit, the tailing and their prisoner; Ham listened to his orders and closed the connection. He waited a while, knowing that the wait would play on their prisoner's mind, and he wanted to give the general time to work his magic. Ham wondered fleetingly if he could manage what the general seemed to do so effortlessly, the wheeling-dealing of high-level politics and intrigues.

Ham decided what he was going to do meantime and how he intended to do it. He got up off the bed, had another quick chat with Jaimie and sent him to the kitchen. After a short word with Rob, he walked back into the kitchen. The prisoner's eyes followed him as he walked in and stood in front but far enough away to avoid any kicking or lashing out of feet.

To Jaimie, he said, "Tie his left foot to the chair in front of the boards." The man began to struggle and tried to speak behind the tape. A clout on the back of the head from Paterson stopped his struggling, but the man breathed heavily, sweated profusely and stared at Ham with bulging eyes.

Ham went over to the table, picked up the pistol, a point 22, and the suppressor and began to screw the suppressor onto the end of the pistol's barrel. The prisoner followed his every move. It was a bit of overkill in the drama department, but it seemed to have the desired effect. All the time, Ham looked deadpan at the prisoner. Ham handed the pistol to Jaimie and hunkered down in front of the prisoner, who followed his every move with his panic-stricken eyes. Ham made a pretend pistol with his hands and aimed it at the man's ankle. Satisfied, he stood up.

"You'll have to get a bit low, but you can get the ankle and the boards behind in a pretty safe shot. I don't think it will go through to the floor. I hope not; I've just had them replaced after the last time. I know…" Ham paused for dramatic effect. "Hold on; I have an idea." Ham walked over to the freezer and took out a fair-sized frozen leg of lamb. Closing the freezer, he placed the meat behind but slightly to the side of the man's leg. "That should do it. You'd better stand away in case there is a ricochet; it's still quite solid," he said to Paterson calmly. Paterson moved in front of the man and stood with his arms crossed, looking disinterestedly at the man's plight from Ham's side. The man was mumbling hard behind the tape.

"My dear fellow, I haven't asked you a question yet. Control yourself. Now, do you want to talk to me?" The man nodded vigorously. "I do hope so, as you will only get one chance. If I ask my colleague to remove your gag, will you talk to me? Please don't waste my time; that would be a waste of my time and could be very painful for you. Are you ready? Now, do you prefer slowly or quickly?" Ham asked as he held the end of the tape gagging the prisoner. Before the man could mumble a reply, Ham whipped the tape from his mouth. It probably took some of his facial hair away, and judging by the loud yelp, it seemed to be a rather painful experience.

"Simple question to begin. At stake is your left ankle, so be honest now. What is your name, and as a follow-up question to save time, for who do you work? I know that's two questions, but what can I say? I cheat. Real name, mind you, not some made-up thing. I already know who you work for, but I want confirmation. I've got to be honest; I don't mind if it costs you your foot." Ham waited. The man stared angrily at Ham. "Ok, let's be dramatic," Ham turned to Jaimie, "I shall count to three, no five, let's make it interesting. When I say five, you shoot. Try not to hit my floor. Hang on; I don't want blood spatter everywhere." Ham walked behind the man and dug into a cupboard. He returned with a towel which he folded a few times in front of the ankle. "That's better. Now, I am not going to repeat my question. One. Pause. Two. Pause. I say this is even more dramatic than I thought it would be. Where was I? Ah yes, three."

"You can't do this!" the man shouted.

"Oh, do quieten down. If I put the gag back on, you won't be able to talk, and I won't be able to hear your answer. You know, I really would prefer you answer my question." Pause. "Poor brave fellow, four. Ham signalled Jaimie, who got down on his knee while drawing a bead on the man's ankle. Jaimie could have hit his target without the show, but he understood what Ham was doing to the prisoner's mind. Paterson slapped the gag back on the prisoner's mouth as the man stared at Jaimie. "Five." Two muffled explosions were drowned by the noise of the wooden and metal boards and frozen meat, shattering, tearing and exploding. The man fell over, screaming into his gag. Princess exited the room at light speed. Ham was happy with the result. Paterson waited until the prisoner stopped trying to shout, looked down at the young man, placed his finger to his lips and removed the gag from his mouth and raised him upright.

"Dammit, that wasn't a good idea putting the towels in front of his ankle; you missed it completely." Ham picked up the leg of lamb and showed it to Jaimie. "Look what you did to my lamb. I was going to cook that at the weekend." Ham made sure, while not making it evident that the prisoner saw the frozen meat remains. Ok, set up the backstop; let's do it again. No count down this time, no games. When I say send it, you take his ankle out, understood?" Jaimie nodded.

"I'm with six!" the man shouted. "Don't shoot. I'm with MI6. Johnstone, Philip Johnstone."

"Ok, who is your boss here? Who is in charge outside?" A slight pause until Johnstone realised the futility of his situation.

"I can't give you his name," Johnstone stated stoically, jutting his chin forward heroically.

"Ok, describe him? Hair and clothes will do." Johnstone replied, and Ham told Paterson to go down with Rob and bring Johnstone's boss up to the apartment.

"What about him?" Jaimie asked.

"Leave him like that so that his boss can see what he went through. It will be better for you," he said, looking at the prisoner. He asked in a pleasant voice, "Would you like a mug of tea or something stronger?" The man stared back in astonishment.

Paterson and Rob returned moments later with Johnston's boss. He was a casually dressed, well-built, but not muscular, dark-haired man in his mid-thirties. His hazel eyes flashed as his eyebrows shot up when he saw Johnstone, but he recovered very quickly. Ham was impressed with the man's self-control; he could not help but smell the gunpowder in the enclosed kitchen. Paterson bent over and started to pick up the splintered wood and dented metal trays.

"What did you do to him?" he demanded calmly, looking at the shattered chopping boards, dented metal trays and now melting shattered frozen meat.

"Would you like a mug of tea, or would you prefer a cup?" Ham asked innocently in reply. He turned to Jaimie, "You can cut our friend loose and make him a brew or whatever. You know where the whatever is." Jaimie nodded. "All of you stay in the kitchen. Open the window; it smells like a firing range. You," looking at the boss, "what's your name?" Johnstone's boss hesitated. "Ok, have it your way, James Bond, follow me." Ham's team smirked as he walked out of the kitchen into the living room. Followed by 'James Bond'

'James Bond's man sniggered when his boss's back was turned. "You guys don't know the half of it," he said quietly to the team. The team looked back, puzzled. "You'll see if I read your boss right."

Political Manoeuvres and Backstabbing

"Call your people downstairs. They are wasting their time and brainpower thinking about how to storm this place and save the pair of you. You can expect a phone call soon. We might as well make ourselves comfortable while we are waiting." Ham sat in his usual corner of the sofa and indicated either the other end or the armchair. "Call them, please; I want to avoid any unpleasantness." The MI6 boss spoke into his hidden mike and looked up. "Please be so kind as to remove your comms equipment, switch it off, of course, and lay it on the table. We have things to discuss to which your team should not be privy. When he was finished, Ham asked, "Do I have to keep calling you James, or will you give me your real name? I'll know soon anyway."

"Who are you people? I know you are Colonel Hamilton, but...."

"If we are going to bandy rank about, it's Lieutenant General Hamilton, if you please." Ham interrupted politely. The man looked surprised. For a fleeting moment, Ham enjoyed his discomfort. To go against a colonel was nothing but a lieutenant general;

that was another matter. Maybe having the rank was not a bad thing after all.

"Who are you? Who do you work for?" The man asked. Ham mused for a moment.

"Sorry, it's above your pay grade, your boss's and probably their boss's too. Let's just say that we both work for the Queen."

"There's no record anywhere about you or your team apart from a notice in the system that says, 'Hands Off'.

"So why didn't you keep your hands off?"

"I was told to find out more about you?" Ham stared at the man. Ham opened his palms as if to say, 'well?' The MI6 man continued, "Who are you, what are you?"

"Look, I could show you a dozen or so different IDs, all of which will check out, but believe me, it's best just to leave it alone. Now, going back to your name, I can continue to call you James Bond, or you can tell me who you are. If you lie and make something up, I'll know within the hour, so that would be a waste of breath." The man hesitated. Ham waited. "Well, James?"

"Croig"

"That's an unusual name, but I see no issue with that. Why were you so hesitant?" The man hesitated again. Ham waited again; it was becoming annoying. Ham raised his eyebrows questioningly.

"Daniel Croig," came the defiant reply. Ham could swear he heard a suppressed snigger from the kitchen.

"Daniel Croig! You have got...." More muffled giggles from the kitchen. "Where's my bloody tea? Get a grip!"

"I was Daniel Croig way before that actor took on the James Bond role. Can you imagine what I have had to put up with? Ah, Croig, Daniel Croig, do come in." Ham decided to stop the banter and get down to business.

"Ok, Daniel, who sent you to us?" Ham held up his left hand, his palm facing Croig. "Save me having to wait until my boss speaks to your director, who will speak to your boss's boss. I want to know, who, and I want to know why?" It was a big decision for Croig, and Ham gave him time to think. "While you're at it, I want to know why Six is in Five's territory. Five looks after issues on home turf, you're the ones swanning around drinking martinis in Monte Carlo and the like. Does Five know that you are working on home territory? They can get rather testy about that, you know."

Of Birds and Vampires

Before Croig could answer the questions, his mobile phone rang, followed a few seconds late by Ham's.

"You talk in here; I'll go next door. I'll be back." Croig picked up his phone and tapped the screen to answer. Ham left him to it.

Ham closed the living room, kitchen, and bedroom doors. Sitting on the bed, he answered the call. It was the general, of course.

"I've spoken to 'C', he's denied all knowledge, and I tend to trust him on this. I think this is something that one of his underlings has come up with trying to gain 'smarty points'. I think it is safe to say that the shit is rolling downhill. Knowing Six, it will probably end up stuck to the chap you've got there."

"That could work to our advantage," said Ham. "I've noticed this chap Croig's life force. He is a Boundary Walker, and I'll bet any money you want he doesn't know it. He's got skills we could use, but…. Of course, he is MI6. There is no getting around that. But if Six are going to plonk the blame on him and kick him out or post him to the back and beyond, we may be able to use him. But Six…." Ham sighed. "We've never recruited from them before, dangerous."

"You're going to be taking over from me soon; what would you do?"

"Son of a bi….." Ham managed to stifle his comment before its completion.

"I'm serious. How would you handle it? If they cut him loose or punish him, do we want him?" Ham thought about it for a moment.

"Let's wait and see what Six does with him. Somebody is talking to him now. They could be telling him his martini allowance has been cut, or his next posting is Greenland. Seriously, if they try to blame him, please push further to find out who the real culprit was and why. I'll talk to him, and we'll take it from there. I think he may be just what we are looking for."

"Macduff is on her way home. The Canadians have taken charge of Ives. We'll see what pans out there. There was another incident in the highlands with some hikers and the Baobhan Sith. Those bloody Vampires are a pain in the arse and need reminding about the contract. They know the consequences if they break the contract. You are going to split your team as we discussed?"

"Yes, Macduff will take a team out to catch or kill them. I think it may have to be terminal. I'll discuss it with Macduff when she's back."

"I've had confirmation from the Norwegians on what the ravens said, the Elves want our help again, and they are asking for Paterson."

"Even though they put him on a death sentence if he ever sets foot in Scandinavia again?"

"The Elf King is graciously willing to pardon Paterson if he agrees to accept the mission." The sarcasm in General Maxwell's voice was not lost on Ham. "If he doesn't go and succeed in his mission, there could be an all-out war between the Elves and the Trolls. Not only bad for them, but it could easily overflow and affect the humans. Bad for those humans directly affected, but it could open the eyes of the general populace that Trolls and Elves exist. Once the Genie is out of the bottle, it cannot go back in."

"I'll go with Paterson as I know the way." Ham waited. There was a pause, and he knew why.

"If anything happens to you, there's no one to replace me. I'm not sure that you should."

"Until such time as I have trained my successor and you've trained me to be yours, we have no choice. Paterson is a good operator, but he's not a Boundary Walker, although I may be wrong on that. He may be, but I don't see it because it is so deep inside him. It would be good if he is. He would be an asset. Don't worry; I'll work on getting Macduff up to speed after these missions." The conversation ended, and Ham returned to a very unhappy looking Croig.

"So, what is it, forced resignation or Greenland?"

"Greenland? No, but just as bad, Bodø, in northern Norway." Ham tsked and looked sad for him; Croig seemed so pitiful. Ham could not help it; he grinned inwardly.

"Yes, I know Bodø. I've been there a few times. Very cold. How do you fancy a change of job?" Croig looked up at him, a confused, comically sad look on his face.

"Don't rub it in," moaned Croig.

"I'm perfectly serious. You'll retain your Civil Service pay, pensions and whatever benefits you have, but you will be working for us."

Ham saw a glimmer of light in Croig's eyes. He was thinking of taking the bait, but Ham wanted him to understand the full implications of taking the lure. "There, of course, is a catch." Croig looked into Ham's eyes and waited. "It's a fresh start. You must leave MI6 behind you. You cannot join us and run back telling tales to Six. That would be a terminal mistake. Very terminal. What I am saying is no idle threat, you understand." Ham looked as serious as he could.

"Who is we?"

"Not yet. I can tell you it's not gourmet food, martinis, shaken not stirred, and a sexy woman on each arm, it's more, mugs of tea, a bacon roll and some most unusual women."

"They are only sending me to Bod□; it's not the end of the world," said Croig trying to convince himself that it wasn't so bad. "Bod□! Luckily, I'm not married anymore; my ex-wife would throw a hissy-fit if I tried to get her to move there."

"More the warm weather type, huh? Have you been to Bod□?" Ham raised an eyebrow and shivered. Croig winced. Ham reeled in line with the fish wriggling none too enthusiastically on the end. Caught, but he would have to keep an eye on him for a while.

Croig did not know it, but Ham was planning on taking him to Norway, Bodø to be exact.

Return from Canada

When Captain Macduff reported back to Ham the following day, he sent her home with instructions to report back that evening after a long hot shower or bath and sleep. She looked exhausted.

"Seven o'clock. Don't be late; I'll make dinner, a cottage pie. We'll talk while we eat. Janet, of course, can come, but she'll have to bring her own fish." Macduff scowled at Ham. "I'm not being funny, my cottage pie has meat in it, and Janet doesn't eat meat, only fish; she's a Selkie. I wasn't sure when you'd be back, and I don't have any fresh fish in the fridge. Besides, why am I explaining all this to you? I'm a lieutenant general, and you are a mere major?" It took a few moments for that to sink in as Macduff was tired after the trans-Atlantic travelling.

"Lieutenant general? They made you up to a lieutenant general. Wow! When I left, you were a colonel; how did that happen?"

"I met people with influence with the military," he said, simple shrugging his shoulders. She paused, then a light suddenly flickered in her eyes.

"Major! I got my major. Yes!" As she pumped her hand in the air, she realised that another presence in the room was looking puzzled at her excitement. "Ooh, this is going to cause a problem." Major, sitting at her feet, looked up at her expectantly. "Good lad." She stroked his head and ruffled his ears. Dogs are easy to please. "It's ok, boy, you have a sister, a fellow major, Major." Major looked at her with a puzzled expression. He looked at Ham, appeared to shrug and left the room, his claws clicking on the floor.

"I think the sooner you make lieutenant colonel, the better. Off you go, and I'll see you later. Second thoughts, ask Janet to come as well. She won't mind making her own eating arrangements. There are some developments, and it affects you both."

"I can stay if you want to start now."

"Flying to Canada, handing over Ives, and flying back is tiring enough without the drive back from Brize Norton. I need you to have a clear head. You have your orders. Vamoose. Seven o'clock. Janet can come at seven or eight, whatever suits her best."

Cottage Pie Debrief

Major Macduff reported back a few minutes before seven o'clock. After a long soak in a Radox saturated bath, followed by a good oiling and a facemask, Macduff had slept for most of the afternoon. She appeared bright and relaxed. She informed Ham that Janet would eat at the ladies' safe house and report at eight.

With a large plate of minced beef, onions and baked beans covered with mashed potatoes in front of them on the kitchen table, Ham asked if she wanted a mug of tea or a beer. Macduff declined both but accepted the tomato sauce as was her wont with cottage pie, no matter how well made.

"What happened in Canada?" Ham asked

"We were met at CFB[43] Trenton by Major Kennedy[44] and his team. He sends his regards, by the way. They took us to that same building we went to the last time[45] and strip-searched Ives."

---

[43] Canadian Forces Base
[44] Major Ivor Kennedy of Canadian Intelligence or Int Branch, Ham's Canadian counterpart
[45] See "Blacker than Black Ops" by Deryk Stronach

"How did Ives behave?"

"He was as good as gold. Did as he was told. No issues, but I could sense he was puzzled."

"If he was puzzled then, imagine what he'll feel like when he gets to the valley. And then," Ham urged.

"They gave him a fresh set of clothes and took us to a medical facility where they gave him a full MRI, CTI scan or whatever it's called. They didn't find anything. What were you expecting that he swallowed a tracker or something like that?"

"Something like that, either swallowed or injected. Six can be pretty devious, and they don't give a damn about who they use and how. So, he was clean, good, what then?"

"He was given a new set of clothes in a sterile environment. They kitted him out with what he needed for a trip to the Headless Valley in the Nahanni Nation Park Reserve. Bouchard[46] took over. He sends his regards as well. Anyway, Bouchard took Ives away. Major Kennedy said he would be taken to the valley

---

[46] Captain Ettiene Bouchard of the CSOR (Canadian Special Operations Regiment) and Macduff's counterpart in the Canadian team.

to see the Shaman. They'll return him when she's finished with him. I caught the next flight back, and here I am.

"Good. How's the food? Not too salty?"

"No, it's good, boss. You should retire and open a restaurant."

"A chance would be a fine thing," Ham told her about his day in London and who he had met. "So, they have promoted me because they want me to take over from the general when he retires. You are probably next in line to take my job as the senior officer, but we need at least three teams, possibly four. We have a terrible habit of losing people on operations, which brings me back to business. Let's clear this lot up before Janet arrives, or she will start fussing. We clear up then relax with a mug of tea. You may want something more alcoholic later; we've got some fun and games ahead. That steep learning curve I've mentioned to you when you started has suddenly gotten a lot more vertical, and we will have new members joining the department shortly. It's going to be fun and games. I'll wash, you dry.

Team Leader Macduff

Janet arrived just before eight as the other two were sipping their mugs of tea.

Once Janet settled down with a glass of water, Ham began the meeting. He told Janet about their promotions, to which she dutifully congratulated Macduff on her promotion to major with a most un-military hug. Ham was a little disappointed that she did not even acknowledge his promotion. He did not want a hug, but a simple, 'Congratulations' would have been expected. Ham's face and manner did not show his disappointment as he continued.

"Right ladies, we are faced with three problems. I think I have the solution to the first and plans of action for the other two." Macduff and Janet looked at him expectantly; even Princess looked over from licking her bum on the windowsill. Major snorted and continued to sleep.

"First problem: the MerKing has asked me, us, to solve the problem of his love-struck daughter. I think I have a solution that could work out well for us in the long term. My suggestion is this; we suggest to the King that his daughter takes human form so that she can see the one she loves in his natural environment." The two women looked at Ham. Macduff chewed her bottom lip a little as she thought. It was Janet who voiced their question.

"How is that going to help Ham?" she asked. Ham leant forward a little as if drawing them in conspiratorially.

"I'm hoping that this dream boy has a wife and kids or at least a steady girlfriend. Macduff, you will pop down and see where the fishing boat docks. You will follow the lad and see where he lives and hangs out. I know it's a bit short, but we can only do this for a couple of days, as we have other pressing matters. We will bring the MerPrincess along to see the lad with other women if you strike lucky. I'm hoping that that will turn her against him. Problem solved," Ham said, opening out the palms of his hands. All that was missing was a 'Taadaa!'

"Won't work," said Janet quietly. Ham and Macduff looked at her.

"Why? What's wrong with my cunning plan?"

"Mermaids are not monogamous. Our little princess will have had many partners. A virgin, she ain't."

"Damn, and I thought it was such a good plan." Ham looked disappointed.

"Fear not, oh great leader, there is some merit in your plan, but not exactly the way you thought." Ham and Macduff looked at the smiling Janet. She saw them looking and laughed. She continued, "When we go to the Indian restaurant, the waiter, what does he smell of?"

"Curry," they both replied together.

"Chinese?" asked Janet.

"Chinese food. Fried usually."

"You smell of stale milk, dairy products to be exact," Janet stated. For Ham and Macduff, the penny was dropping.

"What does a fisherman smell of?" Ham asked Macduff. "She thinks that he smells of fish."

"And what's the first thing he is going to do as soon as he finishes work? Shower or at least clean himself up," she answered herself. "You don't go to a pub smelling of fish. Not the smell for a young man about town should be wearing 'Eau de Poisson'".

"Yes," said Janet, "we need to get the Princess into his local and close enough for her to smell him. Closer, the better. She may not have smelt a dairy smelling freshly scrubbed up human before." Ham was pleased with the conversation; a plan was forming. Macduff still looked a little puzzled.

"Janet, you're a Selkie. Your diet is fish, and you lived in the sea. How come you were attracted to Jack Drummond? He was human and had all the humany smells."

"I saw into his heart. He was a good man. Remember that seals and Selkies are mammals. We have hearts, the same as you. On the other hand, Mermaids are half fish; therefore, they only have half the heart, if any." There was no love lost between the Selkies and Mermaids.

"Ok, I get it; you saw Jack's heart and decided he was a good man, so why are you interested in Ham?" Ham looked at her, horrified. Janet laughed aloud.

"You can still become a second lieutenant, you know Major Macduff," Ham muttered between clenched teeth.

"Sorry, boss. It slipped. Er, moving on, what's the next problem?" Ham looked at the two women for a moment and then shook his head for a moment in exasperation.

Gathering his thoughts, he told them about the encounter with MI6 and Daniel Croig. Macduff could barely control herself when he told her his name. A looked from Ham, and she quietened down. Janet looked puzzled, and Macduff had to explain her problem.

"OK, enough about the history of fictitious characters in MI6. Mr Croig," Ham looked at Macduff, who did not show any more emotion, "is a Boundary Walker, and I think he could be an asset to MIC. The general thinks so too. The general will do some digging and see if he is something we can work with."

"Boss," Macduff started to ask, "how come we send Ives to Canada to see if MI6 tainted him, and yet we are thinking of taking an actual-factual-MI6 man into the fold. We know he is tainted."

"If Ives is tainted, then he was planted with us with the intention of reporting back to Six. We need to know if he was sent to spy on us. Croig is a known quantity. We still need to be careful, but I think he came to us by accident, just like the SBS lads. Happenchance. Hopefully. Don't worry; we will check him out in due course."

"Next item on the agenda, Norway. The Elves have asked that Paterson goes back to Norway to assassinate a Troll King and return his kidnapped Elf 'bride' to the Elves." Ham looked at the pair and continued, "Yes, I know that Paterson is under a death sentence by the Elves if he sets foot in Scandinavia, but I have the Elf King's word that he'll rescind the death sentence if Paterson takes on this task."

"Can we trust this promise? They already tried to kill him."

"Huginn and Muninn, Odin's ravens, brought the King's request to me. That means that he gave his oath in front of them. They do not lie; they are the God's messengers. Under these circumstances, the King also knows that if he goes back on his word and kills Paterson, I will kill him." Ham spoke with a certain finality that Macduff had not heard in his voice before.

"Who's going with him?" Macduff asked.

"Just me, and Major, possibly Croig." Ham could see the looks on Janet and Macduff's faces. "Thank you for your concern, but I am still perfectly capable of a gentle stroll in the Norwegian hills. Anyway, there is another job for the rest of you. You will be dealing with some troublesome Vampires."

"In Romania?" asked Macduff hopefully. "Old castles and romantic Counts. How interesting."

"No, the Highlands of sunny Scotland," said Ham flicking a thumb over his shoulder. "We have our home-grown Scottish Vampires." Ham could see that Macduff was wracking her brain, so he gave her a moment. Ham looked at Janet and could see that she knew.

"The Baobhan Sith!" Macduff suddenly exclaimed.

"Yes, some of the party ladies have reappeared and are up to mischief again. They've been told before of the consequences of their actions. The general says they should have listened." Ham looked at Janet. "It was Jack who agreed the terms of the truce with their leader. I wasn't even in the department at that time. That gives you an idea how long ago they signed the contract and how long they understood and followed the rules."

"A road traffic accident?" Macduff asked[47].

---

[47] See "The Boundary Walker" by Deryk Stronach

"Something like that," Ham replied flatly. "The order is that we send a strong message that will be understood by other members of the clan that are considering leaving the reservation."

"Is this going to be one of those Ops like Paterson's Scandinavian job, where we can't set foot in the Highlands again without being chased by the Baobhan Sith?"

"No, I'm told these 'Ladies' have disobeyed their Chieftain and have gone rogue. There won't be that kind of problem." After a while, he quietly added, "I hope." Both the ladies heard but did not say anything for a time.

"Macduff broke the silence, "Why Croig? Won't he be a liability? As you said, you don't even know if he is safe."

"Then we will just have to find out, won't we?" Ham got up and looked out of the window. "I'll take Major for a little walk down to the Pencil Monument with Janet and hopefully arrange with the king for his daughter to come to us. Alison, there's no need for you to come along tonight. Go, get a good night's sleep. Tomorrow, you start looking for lover-boy and track his habits. Let me know when you have something." Macduff stood up and made to go.

As she left, she turned, smiled and cooed, "You pair have a nice moonlit walk."

"Major!" Ham barked. Major, the dog, jumped up. Ham groaned. Macduff left giggling. Major looked confused.

"Janet, you'd better get your skin. We'll go when you get back. I'll get one of the lads to cover us."

A King Gives up his Daughter

"Yes, I find you extremely attractive, but it just would not work. You are Jack's widow, and you look twenty-eight. I am sixty-six and look, or at least feel eighty. Let's not talk about it, please." They looked at each other for a while and eventually decided to look out to sea.

"Did you agree on a time?" Janet asked after a while.

"Not specifically, because I did not know what was going to happen in London at that point. I did have it at the back of my mind that I would be retired again. I was not expecting a promotion or promotions." Ham stared out to sea for a while longer. "We'll give him fifteen minutes; then, I'm afraid you're in for an evening's swim."

Ham had called the men's safehouse and got Rob. He's asked him to cover them on their walk. Ham never saw him, which was as it should be. Better safe than sorry. Ham believed that Maddox was off to the wilds of Canada, but that did not mean that he or his organisation would not try something funny. Also, there could be other players that Ham was not aware of at that time. The problem with being a member of MIC is that you have many enemies, very few friends and a lot of unknowns.

Just as Ham was about to ask Janet to go into the water and hunt for the MerKing, a ripple appeared in the water nearby.

"You have brought a Selkie with you," the King stated. "My wife said you had a Selkie as your woman." Ham groaned inside but outwardly ignored the comment.

"If you had not turned up, I would have sent her to find you."

"The Mer-people do not get on well with Selkies. You know this."

"I'm sure the feeling is mutual, but we need to work together. I have a plan, but I need to know some answers first." Ham could see the King nod in the dim light.

"Am I right in saying that Mermaids can change into human form at will?"

"Yes," I can arrange that.

"You and your wife's human top half have pale blue skin, and you have green hair; is that also true about your human form?"

"The colour of the skin and hair is a matter of choice. When we are in the depths, our skin darkens. If I had not changed my skin colour, you probably would not see me now. Why do you ask these questions? How does this help my problem with my daughter?"

"I would like your daughter to take human form and colouring and join my people for a while." The King did not stir or say anything. "I believe that once she sees the human youth in his natural habitat that she will turn away from him. Once that is done, I would like her to stay with my team for a while." Ham felt and sensed more than saw the King's discomfort. "She would, of course, be free to return to the sea any time you or she wishes." Ham waited. He wondered if he had pushed too hard too quickly. Maybe he should have gotten her on land with the team before mentioning it to her father.

"I have many sons and daughters. One of them will take over the throne when I am gone. They are sensible and smart. This one is the most troublesome yet winsome one; she is also my favourite. I would not see her hurt. I understand that the work you do is dangerous. We know what you did for the Kelpies and other creatures. I will send her to you for this matter and a trial period after that.

It will be her choice if she decides to stay or not.   On the other side of the marina is a large sandy bay; I shall bring her there at this time tomorrow. Thank you for your efforts, Lt Gen Hamilton."   How did he know of Ham's recent promotion?   It must be the Cat-woman's work, thought Ham.

"Thank you, Your Majesty."

The Problematic Recruit

"Holy Shit!" exclaimed Macduff. Ham glanced at her but understood the sentiment. Ham quickly realised that he was glad he asked Rob and John to act as cover somewhere out in the bushes for this meeting, rather than Jaimie. Jaimie might have also exclaimed aloud or given himself away.

A dusky-skinned well-proportioned maiden walked out of the water with pale eyes and short white or yellow hair. The dark light confused some of the colour recognition, but Ham wondered where the Princess's choice of your average human features had come from. She walked casually, in a sensual feline way up to Ham. She was slightly shorter but stood proud in her nakedness.

"I am Princess Megyn, my father, the King, says that I am to come to you and that you will take me to the man I love. I am here, shall we go."

"Not yet, Princess," replied Janet from behind Ham. The Princess glared at Janet.

"I do not take instructions from a Selkie," turning to look at Ham with a wry smile, "even one who is Hamilton's woman."

"You will address me as sir or boss. Janet," Ham tipped his head towards Janet, "is your senior and far more knowledgeable on the way of humans. You will obey her. Alison, who…"

"I refuse!"

"You will not refuse. You have free will. You may turn around and walk back into the water, now or any time in the future. But, if you refuse to obey your superiors while we are on a mission, I will kill you. I have the King's blessing on that." Ham knew that he did not really, or even if he would carry out his threat except in the direst emergency, but he knew that he had to get this spoilt wilful child in order as soon as possible." They stood staring at each other. The Princess glared very well, but she lacked Ham's experience. The Princess broke her glare and looked at Janet, Macduff and Major.

"Am I to obey the dog as well?" she asked sarcastically.

"Major, angry face!" Major opened his jaw and growled through his metal teeth.

"Again, your choice," Ham replied quietly. The Princess again glared at Ham. He looked back with an expression of total indifference. The Princess turned to go.

As she started to take her first step, Macduff said quietly, but loudly enough for the Mermaid to hear, "I've met your, lover boy. He's not too bad. If you are going, I might take him myself. I think I could train him not to want another woman." The Princess stopped. She paused, then turned to face Macduff. She looked angry but not mad. Macduff leant over to Janet and took a bundle containing a towel, some clothes and a pair of trainers. With these, she walked over to the Princess and held them out. The Mermaid looked at them, at Macduff, who looked pleasantly back at her and took the clothes.

"A track-suit! Really! Did she choose this for me?" the Mermaid exclaimed, looking at Janet.

"No, I did," replied Macduff, calmly lying through her teeth. "They'll do until we can get other clothes that fit for you. We didn't know what shape or size you would be. You're about my size; maybe you might like some of mine until we can go shopping for something better." The Princess nodded thanks and walked over to a large rock where she placed the clothes and dressed.

"Somebody needs to tell the little Princess how to use that towel. When we get back, you need to get her into a bath or shower to get rid of that smell. She smells like old fish."

"Now, now Janet. Let's not have racial tension in the team between Selkies and Mermaids. We are all one happy family."

"I'm smiling, aren't I?"

"No," replied Macduff and Ham in unison.

"Oh, I thought I was," came Janet's voice through her teeth.

The Princess strode back to the group where Ham threw sticks for Major to fetch.

"We play that game with seals," the Mermaid said sweetly, turning to face Janet.

"Yes, the seals think that you are very careless and always losing things, so they are being kind to you," Janet cooed back. The two stared at each other. Ham would have to talk to them individually, or maybe better get Macduff to do it. He signalled to Macduff to come closer.

"Once you get her settled, pop over for a chat. Just you," he added with a knowing look.

"Yes, boss."

"Ok, ladies! Let's head back. You go back to your place and clean up. I'll see everyone at the Indigo Eats tomorrow at ten or eleven if you can reserve the back room for us. If it's busy and it's a nice day, we'll take the ferry across to Cumbrae and have a nice group chat somewhere along the shoreline, somewhere nice and quiet. If the weather is against us, you three can go shopping for clothes. We have a great budget but don't break the bank. That's the plan, but things change. Ok, lead on Mac…." Macduff glared at Ham, and he smiled back. "After you ladies."

As Ham walked behind the ladies with Major at his heels, he signalled in the general area where he believed John and Rob hid to join him.

"I didn't hear anything so, I guess the coast is clear," he said softly.

"All clear on the ground, boss, but if someone is playing with surveillance drones or something like that…" Rob shrugged his shoulders.

"Yes, we need to consider that in the future. Well, what are your comments on the new addition?"

"I'm glad Jaimie wasn't here to see her grand entrance," said John. "Reminded me of that James Bond entrance on the beach. What was her name?"

"Daniel Craig?" suggested Rob innocently.

"No, you twit! I said her."

"Halle Berry?"

"I wasn't thinking of her, but she is closer. Who was the first? The first Bond film. Doctor No, Sean Connery on the beach and out of the water walks..? Honey, something."

"Honey Rider."

"That's the one. Just like, who was the actress? Ursula Undress, except this one, was without the clothes. Poor Jaimie, he will be upset when he finds out what he missed."

"I believe her name was Andress, Ursula Andress," corrected Ham. "He'll find out soon enough. Have a quiet word with him, the pair of you. We must keep a cohesive team. There's an old expression, 'You don't shit on your own doorstep'. Both of you keep an eye on them. I don't mind if they have a relationship; that might help her join the team, but it must be done maturely. You are all grown men, or so I'm told."

"I agree; Jaimie is too young and inexperienced," mused Rob. "Maybe you'd prefer John, or I proffer ourselves as suitable candidates instead. She is pretty fit. I am willing to take one for the team boss." Ham heard John groan. He may even have let out a small groan himself.

"I don't control my team's lusts and desires but remember that doorstep guys." Ham walked on in silence. He was eager to expand his team, and a MIC team needed diversity to deal with the broad scope of missions, but had he been too keen to take on a Mermaid into a team that already had a Selkie, natural enemies. Rob and John bickered and bantered on the way back to the town. They stopped as they drew nearer to civilisation, and the three walked in silence. Ham was all for fun, sort of, but he was glad to see that the lads knew when to be professional.

Of the ladies, there was no sign. Ham hoped that Macduff could deal with the other two. He decided it was good training for her as a future team leader.

Princess and Prince Charming

"So, how're things going?" Ham asked with a smile.

"Well, I've left the little Princess with Janet. Janet has promised me that the little angel will still be alive by the time I get back. Although I am only willing to take an evens bet on that."

"Problematic? Or should I say too problematic?" Ham asked seriously, "Do you think I made a mistake?"

"No boss, we'll manage, but she is going to be a handful initially."

"For instance?"

"She doesn't want to sleep on a bed. She wants to sleep in the bath. It's too small, but it will do. She prefers salt water, but fresh water will do."

"And the problem is?" Ham asked.

"The bath is ensuite to the larger bedroom." Ham looked blank. Then the light bulb lit up.

"Who has the master bedroom.?"

"Janet."

"Ah, so what is happening?"

"Princess is helping Janet move her things into the third bedroom. I've never seen Janet mutter under her breath so much, not even when you upset her." Ham looked up from his mug of tea at Macduff. Macduff grinned.

"Any other issues?"

"A couple, we asked her what she eats. Like Janet, she prefers sea food." Ham looked at her quizzically.

"She will also eat small mammals or birds if she gets a chance." A short pause before she continued. "Major can take care of himself, but Princess might be too much of a temptation. I would keep them separated initially." Ham nodded.

"And the second problem?"

"She's eager to meet her beloved. I've agreed with Janet that we will monitor her until we judge the right time. I slipped a camera into her room. She'll never know it's there. Do you want to see?" Macduff held up her phone. Ham back away, horrified.

"I'm not in the habit of spying into a lady's bedroom. It's not right. I don't like it."

"You, old prude you. Anyway, she's no lady," Macduff laughed.

"You old prude you, sir," Ham replied huffily. I shall leave that area up to you but keep me informed if there are any problems. Once we know she will not abscond, you take it out. Clothes?"

"She is wearing my clothes. They fit her disgustingly well, especially my good stuff. If we can, we'll take her shopping tomorrow, then we'll be ready to introduce her to the world, and God help it."

"It sounds like you are not impressed, Alison."

"She's just a bit immature, bold, demanding. But to be honest, she's new to this living with the human's thing. I'm surprised her English is so good. Janet says it's because mermaids listen to people on anchored ships and from underneath piers and the like. It takes brains to learn a language just by hearing it. She must be smarter than she looks. Janet calls her Migraine. Megyn hasn't cottoned on. There will be fireworks when she does." Macduff smirked a little.

"In other words, she's young. You think she will fit?" Macduff thought for a few moments.

"As long as she doesn't do or say something to blow our cover in the early stages, I think she could be moulded into someone useful. Yes, I think she'll be alright eventually. But the next few days are going to be tricky. We have to control her impulses."

"Right," said Ham; if you want to go shopping uptown tomorrow, we'll cancel the breakfast meeting. I'd better brief you on your upcoming mission so that you can prepare for it. A mug of tea, and we will start." Macduff's eyes rolled.

Ham sipped his steaming mug a few moments later and looked at Macduff.

"You know what a bothy is?"

"An old hut or cottage, normally stone, no electricity, water or sewerage. They are dotted around the wilds of Scotland. Free to use. Just leave it as you found it. If someone beats you to it and they don't want to share, you sleep in your tent outside."

"Good, fair description. Anyway, a few hikers, walkers and the like have either disappeared or turned up badly gored with their necks ripped out. If this had happened somewhere like the wilds of Alaska or Canada, they would have put it down to bears or wolves.

However, we don't have bears or wolves here, but what we do have are Baobhan Sith." Ham looked at Macduff, who nodded. "Baobhan Sith are often called Scottish Vampires. Tall, slim, beautiful ladies, normally dressed in long green dresses, deer-like hooves instead of feet, but the dresses normally hide these. To attract them, you need music to dance by and a statement made by a male saying that he wished there were women present in the Bothy. They appear, they dance, and when they are ready, they pounce. A mouthful of teeth that would make a Hollywood special effects artist proud materialise where those pearly whites had been, and they start chewing away. They are after the blood, but they are not fussy about the method of getting it. No napkins, if you get what I mean. When they are sated, they go."

"Now, two things you need to know, one is that they cannot stand iron. Normal bullets or silver, anything like that, will have no effect—only iron. There is a legend of three young men attacked in a bothy by the Baobhan Sith; only one lived to tell the tale because he ran out of the hut and cowered between their horse's feet. It shows you how old that legend is. The horse's iron horseshoes protected him. And two, we have had an agreement with the Baobhan Sith leadership that they will not attack humans. It seems that two, possibly three, have gone back to the old ways. Their leader has agreed that they need to be made an example of before others join or copy them. Their leader and General Maxwell have agreed that their example should be terminal. Do you understand what I am saying?"

"Yes, boss," was all Macduff replied. Ham got up and retrieved a large envelope from the safe. He handed it to Macduff.

"Here are the details, the location of the affected bothies, maps of the other bothies in that area. Take Jaimie and Rob as bait. You, Janet and Megyn, will spring the trap. You take care of the logistics, plan the ambush, and decide who does what. The boys may not want to deal with women, or should I say, creatures that look like women. I know they are roughy-toughy special forces guys but keep that in mind. If the Baobhan Sith escape, they will kill other people. Later on, tell me how Megyn behaves. If I can get him onto the team in time, I'll give you Daniel Croig as extra bait. Throw him in the deep end and see how he reacts."

"When are you off with John?" Macduff asked.

"Any time, just waiting for a phone call from the general's ever-reliable PA Ms Miller to say that arrangements have been made in Norway. I've asked John to join me later when we take Major for his nightly walk. I'll brief him as much as I can then. If you can quickly sort out the fisherman lover boy and the Vampires, come across Norway with Rob and Jaimie. Leave the Mermaid Princess with Janet; there won't be any water where we are going. Ask Ms Miller for details and ask her to make the necessary arrangements if you get the chance. You decide whether to bring Mister Croig or not. See how he behaves. I think it's going to be a messy one. This job will be one of the more, the merrier ones. Trolls are very stubborn and belligerent at the best of times, but going into their underground Kingdom, is asking for trouble. If things do go to rat-shit, you may find yourself promoted quicker than you thought." Ham smiled at her. "I did warn you that there was a steep learning curve."

"You're taking Major and Princess with you? I'm thinking of the Mermaid's dietary habits. She can't go with us."

"Major, yes, he'd be an asset. Trolls and wolves don't mix well, so he'll be ok. But Princess is another matter, Trolls like small mammals, and I don't mean as pets. She can't remain with you because of Megyn, and she can't come with us, and the general has said no before to looking after the beasts, that only leaves one person."

"Who?"

"Return to sender, at least temporarily, the Guardian. I don't know how she knows, but she knows when to appear. Go for a few walks and hope that she appears. I'm betting that she will. Megyn will eat the same as Janet; check with her. Now, I think you have left Janet and her prot□g□ long enough for their first night together. You had better be off."

"You want another mug, boss?"

"No thanks, Alison," said Ham standing up and looking at his watch, "I'd better be off out with Major and Princess. Oh Alison, one last thing, when these present missions are over, remind me to send you down to London, to the MIC Library. I think you need to read up on our illustrious history. A couple of weeks will do for the first visit. We'll take it from there."

A Surprise Reunion

It was the afternoon of the second day that Ham, Paterson and Major flew courtesy of a Royal Norwegian Air Force C-130J-30 transport aircraft to the northern coastal town of Narvik.

Ham had spoken to Macduff before departure, and she said they would make their first attempt that night to bring the Mermaid Princess Megyn and her heart's desire together, hopefully with disastrous results. Ham hated to think what he would do if the Princess was still enamoured of her love interest after the encounter. Ham did not have a plan B yet.

Macduff said she had made discrete enquiries of the fisherman's routine. Therefore, she, Janet and Megyn would follow the fisherman from the fishing boat home and then wait nearby until later; hopefully, once he had cleaned up and kissed his wife and kids goodbye, he would go out for his routine evening's entertainment. They would probably follow him on to the pub he usually frequented. She said Rob and Jaimie would run discrete security for them. Macduff said she would keep him posted on developments.

There was something in Macduff's voice that made Ham think that she was holding something back. When he had asked her, she said it was something she had only thought of recently and would confirm tonight. She said she was not sure how it would pan out. She said Croig had not turned up. Ham replied that the general was working on it and that if Croig was transferred to them, Ms Miller would let her know.

Macduff finished the call with, "Anyway boss, safe journey boss, and maybe see you in a couple of days. Watch yourself with those Elfin women." Truer words are often spoken in jest to the wrong person.

As Ham, Paterson and Major stepped off the aircraft, they were greeted by the Norwegian team, all of which they had met before. The leader of the team was Major Magnus Munsen, Sersjantmajor[48] Mathias Berland, both members of the FSK, Forsvarets Spesialkommando, Norwegian Special Forces. Mathias was not your typical imagining of the tall blond-haired, blue-eyed Viking; he was a northern Norwegian, dark-skinned, dark-haired and dark-eyed and, to use a very

---

[48] Norwegian sergeant major

British description, built like a brick shithouse. Luckily an ever-present smile topped his solid menacing frame. However, the third member of the Norwegian team shocked at least one of the British team, Løtnant Talya Johansdotter of the Royal Norwegian Navy, the Sjøforsvaret. She glowered at the Brits as they descended the aircraft's ramp. Ham smiled back; he knew the glower was not aimed at him.

During a previous mission to Norway[49], John Paterson had assassinated two Dark Elves at the behest of the Scandinavian Elf King. Even though this was carried out at the request of the Elves, a sentence of death had immediately been placed on Paterson's head any time he was found within Scandinavia. No one is permitted to kill an Elf. During his escape from Norway on a Royal Norwegian Navy ship, Talya, an Elf in human form, had attempted to drown him, thus carrying out the King's wishes. Paterson had arrived safely home in Largs a few days later, having

[49] See "Never in Ones" by Deryk Stronach

by luck, been saved from a cold watery grave by some passing and astonished British fishermen. No sooner had he turned up at the Largs safehouse that he shared with the other male team members than Talya turned up. She reiterated the death sentence passed by the Elves but strangely stated that the King was pleased with Paterson's job. Elf logic. He had been used as an Elf cannot kill another Elf. After their second encounter, Paterson and Talya had a brief but heavy romance before he went back to MIC business and she back to the Norwegian Navy. They promised to write and call, but Paterson didn't write and ignored her calls.

He looked at her face and saw that she was not a happy bunny. During the pauses between their lovemaking, they talked of a future together. It was plain on Talya's face that John Paterson may not have taken that seriously, but Talya had. Ham leaned closer to Paterson.

"You don't shit on your own doorstep, remember," he muttered.

"I wasn't expecting to come back to this doorstep again, remember," Paterson replied out of the corner of his mouth. "And I certainly wasn't expecting this welcoming committee."

Major Munsen was unaware of Talya's relationship with the team, especially Paterson. Munsen was also a Boundary Walker and knew that Talya was an Elf; that was part of why he had selected her for his team. He noticed the change in atmosphere and raised an eyebrow at Ham.

"We'll talk later. We need to find some decent coffee. Royal Norwegian Air Force coffee is as bad as our RAF muck."

They collected their equipment and walked towards the waiting transport a Royal Norwegian Air Force, or Luftforsvaret, Agusta Westland AW101 helicopter. Munsen congratulated Ham on his rapid promotion and said he wished that the Norwegian Army should follow the British example. Berland and Johansdotter walked ahead. Talya seemed to be overly engrossed in a conversation with Berland. Her body language indicated that it was a false show of casualness. Paterson walked behind them, head bowed, slowly shaking his head side to side. Ham ignored his glances. The walk was short, but Munsen looked at those ahead and then quizzically at Ham, so Ham repeated that he would tell Munsen the whole story when they were alone. It was something the two team leaders needed to discuss. It could cause problems for the mission.

Munsen casually commented that Ham looked younger than when they had last met. There were some matters that Ham could not discuss and replied equally as casually that clean living and a healthy lifestyle and diet were the keys. Ham thought it a good reply until Munsen lent a bit closer and whispered, "My friend, you forget that I am also a what you call a Boundary Walker. I can see." Ham did not miss a step, but he looked at Munsen, who smiled back. "It is good that you do not play poker as you are a terrible liar." Ham smiled back, and they walked on.

Ham was surprised when the Norwegians led them past the aircraft to a nearby building.

"We can have a coffee and chat after you have changed. I know where we are going, but you, Lieutenant General Hamilton, may want to change some of the weapons and equipment once you have seen what I've selected. Of course, I bow to your exalted rank," he added with a laugh, knowing that each had their expertise and would work together to complete the mission.

Settling Differences

Once kitted up and with a mug of good strong coffee in his hand, Munsen took Ham to a small room down the corridor. The room was obviously used as a night duty room or temporary quarters, having a heater, a desk, a chair, a wardrobe and a simple made-up bed in the corner. Munsen offered Ham the seat and sat on the bed. Ham explained the history between Talya and Paterson.

"Do we change the teams? Talya is an Elf, which will be useful, but the Elf King, who I should mention, is her father," Ham groaned, "specifically asked for WO2 Paterson for the mission. How are they going to work together? Special Forces teams need cohesion. Dammit, this makes it awkward," Munsen muttered angrily. "Trolls are bad enough to deal with without this complication." While he spoke, probably since the greeting at the aircraft, Ham had thought what to do.

"Can you get your girl under control? I'll deal with my boy. They're both professionals."

Munsen raised his eyebrows in a gesture that said, "Right, good luck with that." Ham slapped his thighs and stood up.

"Ok, we give them a knife each and lock them in this room for ten minutes. The survivor comes with us."

"And the loser?" Munsen asked with a smirk, knowing that Ham was joking.

"The mortuary or the hospital. Come on." Munsen watched Ham head towards the door. He stood up and quickly followed. As they entered the main room, the rest of the teams looked up expectantly. Even Major stood up, knowing that something was going to happen.

"Right, you two. This needs to be sorted out now, before the mission." Everyone looked at Ham. He looked first at Paterson and then at Johansdotter. "You two, strip." Their eyes opened wider as they continued to stare. Munsen and Berland's heads tilted quizzically. Major juggled his eyebrows and tilted his head. "You heard me correctly, strip naked, now or walk out of that door and off the mission, maybe off the teams." Ham waited. First, Paterson started to undress and then after seeing a slight shrug from Munsen, Johansdotter followed suit. Munsen looked down and checked a list with deep concentration. Berland found something interesting in his kit to examine. When they were completely naked, Ham spoke again.

"Pick up your knives without the sheaths and follow me." He turned and, obviously expecting to be obeyed, left the room, heading back to the room where he had talked with Munsen. He entered the room, they followed, glancing at each other, still slightly puzzled. "You have ten minutes to sort out your problem one way or tother. If you need longer, leave the knives outside the door. If I see the knives, I will leave your clothes. If I don't see the knives, I will leave all your kit, and you will remain here until we return. Transport leaves in thirty minutes with or without you." Ham turned and left, closing the door behind himself.

"I used to have such a good career. I saw myself slowly rising through the ranks until retirement, not a blemish on my record; if word of this gets out, I'll be court-martialled and kicked out, if I'm lucky." He hung his head and groaned. Berland looked at his boss with concern. "Ok, what do we do now?" asked Munsen as Ham sat in the armchair next to him.

"We drink another of these wonderful coffees and wait." Munsen and Berland shrugged as if all was normal. Borland took the mugs and went to arrange their refills.

Halfway through the mug's steaming hot content, Munsen stated, "They might kill each other."

After a sip, Ham replied, "Wanna bet?" Munsen scrunched up his mouth, looked at Ham and then down to the rug on the floor and shook his head. "People don't normally kill people when they are naked," Ham added softly. "I could be wrong, but Warrant Officer Paterson could not hide his interest in resolving their predicament."

"You mean…" Munsen glanced down between his legs and back to Ham. Ham nodded with a smirk.

"Now about that bet?" Ham asked.

"Bad odds. You could be right. I hope you are. I honestly don't know."

After ten minutes, Ham stood up and walked out of the room. As he walked back in, Munsen and Borland looked at him. His face was noncommittal. He held up the two knives; one blade had a little blood on it.

"It looks like they shall survive," was all he said, throwing the knives onto the bundles of discarded clothes. The blade with the blood landed on Talya's clothes. "I guess where we are going, the coffee will not be this good.

Sergeant Major, one last mug if you please and then leave their clothes outside the door, please."

"How do you manage to drink so much coffee?" Munsen asked.

"Dedication and practise," Ham replied with a wry smile. Ham leaned towards Munsen and muttered sweetly, "Still sure you want to play poker with me?"

Munsen humphed in reply.

It was later, as Ham was walking back from the toilet, where he had deposited the rented coffee, that the two lovers returned.

"Ok, get yourselves, cleaned up, kitted up and ready to go in five minutes. We have work to do." The pair gathered their equipment with as much dignity as they could muster and left the room, Talya showing Paterson the way.

Ham leaned into Munsen. "Now we talk to them. Get them back on track." Munsen nodded.

The time waiting for the pair had not been wasted; Ham, Munsen, and Borland had discussed the mission. Ham had been to the Trolls Kingdom once before, as had Munsen, but in his case, many times. They had a fair idea of where they were going and what to expect. Munsen went out to discuss the landing zone with the helicopter pilot, returning a few moments later.

"I'll take Paterson into the room again for a quiet man to man chat. You stay here with Talya and have a man to Elf chat. We need them both with their heads screwed on straight. The Trolls are an unpredictable lot, especially Hugo."

Hugo, the Troll King, was a nasty, cantankerous piece of work, but he could be sensible and persuadable when the mood took him. Ham hoped it would be the latter as he did not want to battle the Trolls. They were formidable foes, especially in their environment. In, talk him into handing over the kidnapped Elf 'brides', and out and away before he changed his mind. That was the plan, but they had other plans, just in case. Trolls could not help being Trolls.

The Gently Sloping Hills of Norway

"You bloody did that on purpose. Now, I'm committed to marrying her. I was tricked. Trapped! Tricked and trapped."

"You bloody did that on purpose, sir," Ham replied softly. Ham waited.

"Sir," Paterson said.

"John, I need you to sort your head out right now. We don't have time for any personal nonsense. You love the girl; that was obvious when I saw the pair of you together in Largs." Paterson looked as if he was about to speak, but Ham raised his hand to silence him. "I know you've told me that you are committed to the job and that you think it unfair for a partner or wife to have to put up with a Special Forces operator always travelling around at short notice and possibly not returning or, even worse, returning injured. You're willing to put your life on the line, but you don't want the responsibility of having a loved one waiting at home while you are off enjoying yourself in harm's way. Talya is also a Special Forces operator; she understands the risks. Two, you may be the one waiting at home for her. Three, if you have promised to marry her, you've committed to marrying her, and the Elves don't take that sort of promise lightly. You try to walk away, and you are a dead duck. Not just in Scandinavia this time, but worldwide. Oh, did I mention that her father is the Elf King? I think you met him the last time you were here. The biggest wolf you had ever seen, you said if I remember correctly. In human form, he's just as big and mean if you cross him."

"Christ, another Princess! That's all we need." Paterson's face froze. "Kerrist! Him! Geez." Paterson remembered his encounter with the Elf King when the King had reluctantly pronounced the sentence of death on Paterson.

"Yes, congratulations, he will be your father-in-law. And just for the record, I didn't tell you to get engaged. That, my boy, was your idea." Ham could see that Paterson's mind was deep in turmoil. "Cheer up, lad; things could get better. You may get killed on the mission." Ham laughed and stood up. "Seriously, John and I mean seriously, she's a beautiful girl, but you need to snap out of it now. You tell me you're ready to go, or I leave you here. Major Munsen is having a similar talk with Løtnant Talya Johansdotter. I, Major Munsen and Sersjantmajor Mathias

Berland will go in without the pair of you if we must understand? If that happens, Janet would never forgive you." Ham left the room. Paterson blinked a couple of times and followed.

After checking their equipment one last time, Munsen mentioned in passing that they had double-checked the gear for tracking devices. It seemed the Norwegian secret service was as curious as their British counterparts. Loading up, the team walked out to and boarded the helicopter, which took off shortly afterwards.

They flew northeast away from the coast and into the mountains through a slight snowstorm. Gentle rolling hills, these were not. Ham was glad that they did not have to traverse them by vehicle or foot. As it was late December, the teams were dressed in warm clothing.

As the helicopter flew on, Major lay with his eyes closed between Ham's feet. He was not asleep; every time the aircraft was buffeted, his eyes opened quickly and closed slowly. The human sat quietly, showing an air of disinterest. Honest or feigned, there was nothing else they could do.

As they drew near the LZ, Landing Zone, Munsen pointed out a lit compound off to their left. It consisted of a large warehouse and what looked like accommodation and offices. All the buildings were close to one another and connected by enclosed walkways. Around them stood a solidly built fence that looked electrified. The complex was built to cope with Norwegian winters; even the watchtowers periodically spaced on the circumference winterproofed. Ham nodded. The others that could see, noted the structure in passing. Hopefully, it was not part of their mission.

Dropping them off on a small plateau, the helicopter took off again into the sunset. The darkness would not bother them where they were going. The hidden cave entrance was about two kilometres away as the crow flies; add another few on top of that if the crow foolishly walked.

As they walked towards the entrance, Ham pointed at the nearby compound a couple of kilometres' distance.

"I don't remember a compound there before. Isn't it a bit dangerous being so near the Troll cave entrance?"

"It's relatively new—a few years. We know about it and have been monitoring it. I'll tell you later. The owner is a very wealthy Norwegian called Nilsen."

Somewhere in the distance, a wolf howled. Paterson looked at Talya.

"Relatives?" he asked half-jokingly.

"Just my father. He was just letting me know he was there. He's very protective." Paterson gulped and smiled back.

They arrived just as the sun set over the mountains. The climb had been steep, and there were no defined trodden paths. If you did not know when to go, you would find it almost impossible to locate. The cave was concealed behind a rocky mount and covered by an overhanging outcrop. Ham was sure that the Trolls had many other entrances, but this was the one Jack Drummond had brought him to many years before. The Norwegian Trolls were usually the Norwegians' problem, but there was a lot of overlap and co-operation between the various countries' teams. Ham knew of three other Troll Kingdoms under the mountains of northern Norway, two in Sweden, one in Finland and possibly some in Russia.

Into the Dark Depths

Ham made one last call to Macduff using his military encrypted sat phone. He didn't need to talk with her, but it gave him a chance to grab a sneaky breather. He was not as young as he used to be. She said she was expecting the fishing boat at any time and had nothing new to report. Packing the phone away, they entered the cave; Berland led the way, using a powerful flashlight. Each carried the same heavy-duty military-grade torches sweeping the area as they walked. Major Munsen followed Berland covering the front left, Talya, the front right, Ham, with Major the centre, scanning all around, with John Paterson bringing up the rear as the tail-gunner. As Paterson entered the cave, he adjusted his bergen or rucksack, so everything sat comfortably and worked correctly.

If Ham and Munsen's memory served them right, the battery-powered torches were only for the initial entry into the cave system; the Trolls lit their domain with flaming torches.

Major sniffed the air and hesitated, looking up at Ham. Ham assured him it was ok and bent down to pat his neck. Placated but not wholly reassured, Major walked by Ham's side, glancing into the shadows and growling in his throat. Ham would whisper words of encouragement to the dog to keep going, although he felt the heavy presence of the dark creatures.

"I know they are there, boy. Good lad. Stay with me, lad. Let's not start anything, eh? Everything alright with you, John?" John knew why he asked, but he cringed at the loudness of his voice.

"They will hear you, boss," muttered Patterson under his breath, who could not understand why the boss was making so much noise.

"It's ok, John, they knew we were here even before we entered the cave. This is their area, inside, outside, all around, and God help any man or beast who wanders in accidentally."

"What about women?" Talya asked. Ham could not tell if she was being flippant or serious.

"That's why we are here, Talya; Trolls have a liking for women, Elf women especially. Look on the good side; if we fail, we will be on the menu, and you will find yourself married to a Troll."

"How is that the good side?" she asked, still focussing on the shadows and the path ahead.

"You won't have to marry John," Ham replied. If she could have seen in the dark, she would have seen Ham's deadpan face. John Paterson grunted in the darkness.

After several twists and turns, burning torches stood out from the walls at head height. They switched off their torches and followed the path. There were other tunnels leading off their route, down which Ham could hear mutters and scrapes. He knew the team was being directed down into the mountain; Ham assumed to meet the Troll King. He was the only one who made decisions; his word was law in his domain.

They marched into the lion's den, except the Trolls were far worse than the King of the jungle. The Trolls claimed to be Kings of the mountain caves, disputed by their only natural enemies, the Dwarves. At that moment, Ham wished he had some Dwarves on the team. Major kept turning to look behind. Ham calmed him down with soothing words and told him to ignore the sounds. Major walked on with the others, but his ears kept twitching and scanning.

The team marched on, down into the depths. The air became foul. The others might have thought it was the smoke from the burning torches or the damp dripping walls and ceilings. The air became heavier as they descended but still breathable. Air was being drawn in or pumped in and circulated somehow, as the torches still burnt brightly.

"We've passed a lot of torches, boss; how do they keep them going? Or are they there just for us?"

"This evening's illumination comes courtesy of the Troll King," answered Major Munsen. "He wants us to follow the yellow brick road. Normally, the torches are more spread out, covering the other tunnels. As for how they are lit? Let us just say the Trolls have lived here for hundreds if not thousands of years. Each generation digging wider and deeper. At some point, they hit oil. The Trolls probably have bigger oil reserves than most OPEC[50] countries."

---

[50] OPEC – The Organization of the Petroleum Exporting Countries. Made up of 15 South American, African and Middle East countries.

"Does the Norwegian government know the oil is here?" Talya asked.

"I may have forgotten to mention that in my reports," answered Munsen. "The general knows, but he also knows that if the humans tried to get it, by humans I mean the politicians and oil companies, I will call them human for this explanation, there would be an all-out war with the Trolls, and I'm not sure who would win." Munsen could hear the intake of breath as Talya prepared to speak. "The navy and air force are no good down here, and I'm not sure the army could beat the Trolls on their home turf. There would be a lot of casualties for an uncertain end. Anyway, we have enough oil for the time being." They lapsed into silence and marched on through the labyrinth of caves and tunnels.

"The Troll King told Jack Drummond that if the humans tried to get the oil, part of the Trolls' battle plan would be to defend the tunnels and make any invader pay heavily. Then they would counter-attack by collapsing the entire cave system and moving up onto land to fight there, killing and destroying everyone and everything in their way. You see, you can fight Trolls, kill Trolls and that is not a problem, but try and take what is theirs, and they get rather upset. Short and sweet, you can kill them but steal from them, and you piss them off. It's a weird Troll logic."

"John, do you want to stop for a break?" Ham called back.

"No, boss, I'm good for a while yet. I don't know how far we have yet to go. Better wait."

"Feeling tired, John?" Talya asked sweetly. John muttered under his breath.

"Now, now Lötnant Johansdotter, let the man do his job," muttered Munsen. He could not see in the dark, but a questioning look passed over Talya's face.

A Guide

After a while, they stopped for a rest, and John fiddled around with his bergen. Talya started to get up, but Munsen placed a hand on her arm.

"He's fine. Don't draw attention to him," he muttered quietly. "Just sit, rest and eat your rations." Talya did as she was told.

They all heard movement in the dark outside the range of the nearby lit torches.

"Why you stop?" came a deep growling voice. "The King is waiting for you. Do not keep the King waiting," the voice commanded.

"We humans are weaker than you. We need rest and nourishment. You understand nourishment?" said Ham tiredly. "We drink, we eat, we go. I'm sure the King does not want us harmed," pause, and then quieter so that only the others could hear, "yet."

"Hurry up," came the growl from the dark.

"Sargant Major Berland. How are your coffee skills down here?"

"I just so happen to have the mixings right here. Anybody else?" They all muttered assent.

"What are you doing? What is he doing?"

"He is making medicine. As I said, humans are weak."

"Hurry up!"

"How far to go? He needs to know how strong to make the medicine."

"All done, boss," Paterson muttered.

"Good," Ham replied softly.

"If there were a shorter way, we would get to the King quicker," Ham called out. Quieter, he said, "They've been leading us around to get us disorientated. I'm getting tired of this bullshit."

"I have been here before; I know that you are lighting tunnels to take us the long way to your King. We will take our medicine," he said, taking a sip and groaning with pleasure, "and then rest. We cannot go all over the place for your pleasure. I shall complain to the King." There was a pause. It became more than a pause as it grew longer. Trolls were not the most intelligent creatures, and it took a bit of time for the Troll to decide what to do.

"You take your medicine, and I take you to see King."

"Good, but I feel weak and in need of more medicine."

"Hamish!" squawked Munsen in exasperation.

"Ok, ok. Let me finish this, and then we'll go." A few minutes later, they had cleared away and were ready to go. "Ready when you are? Lead the way."

A huge grey-green, almost reptilian skinned creature, muscular, vaguely human in appearance in that it had two arms, two legs, a body and a head, stomped past them. The creature did not appear to have a neck attached to the square-shaped body. Its ears were large and pointed, as was its head. Its eyes were large, dark, showing almost no white; they sat above a large round flat nose, bulging out from a face that not even a mother would love. The mouth did not appear to have lips but held two sets of razor-sharp yellow teeth, but fangs might be a better description. They had never seen a toothbrush, and even as the creature passed a meter or so away, Ham could smell its evil-smelling breath above the rank body odour.

They followed.

"What's your name?" Ham asked pleasantly. Yet another pause as it processed this question.

"Ingrid," she replied.

"Oh Geez," muttered Paterson.

"Now, now John, control yourself; you are nearly a married man," Ham said calmly.

"Why he says, this Geez? I speak your language good. What does it mean?"

"He was praying to his God. He is a very religious man." Ingrid shook her head and stomped on.

"I warn you, I virgin," Ingrid growled. Ham heard Paterson whimper. Munsen laughed.

"She means she has not killed a human yet."

"Thank God for that!" gasped Paterson.

"It is a rite of passage for Trolls," explained Ham. "Kill a human; you move up the hierarchy. Don't worry, John, I think your virginity is safe."

"You virgin too?" Ingrid asked seriously.

"Yes," answered Paterson weakly.

"Lying bastard," muttered Talya.

His Regal Majesty

The audience chamber was massive by any standard. Although Ham had seen it before, he marvelled at the size and construction. It seemed bigger. Maybe they had added to it. It stood about eight to ten stories high, with balconies cut into the rock up to the dark ceiling. Ham guessed that there was a ceiling, but the top was obscured with dark forbidding clouds. Many burning torches dotted the walls, their yellow light flickering on the embedded semi-precious stones and metals.

On a dais stood a large gold throne and, on the throne, sat the Troll King, Hugo, as they were to discover. Troll Kings change with monotonous regularity, bloody coups being the standard mode of transition of Kingship.

Hugo, the present King, wore a filthy grease-stained leather kilt and a large diamond-studded gold chain around his neck. The chain was his only symbol of status, but his bearing as he looked down at Ingrid, showed everyone present on the floor and the crowded mass leaning out over each of the balconies, who was in charge. The King did not need a crown; he was the King. Two larger than average Trolls stood behind the King, large scimitar like swords hung from their thick leather belts, automatic rifles, looking like toys in their large hands. They could not even get their fingers in the trigger guards. Giant black talon-like fingernails rested on the triggers. Standing just out of the shadows, others held metal and wood spears. The last time Ham had visited the Kingdom, admittedly many years before, the weapons had been cruder with the weapons made of crudely carved wood and stone blades. Ham wondered if the Trolls had advanced technologically naturally or got the armaments elsewhere. He knew the answer to his question, even before it entered his head. Who would trade with the Trolls? Trading with Trolls was a hazardous occupation strictly controlled by the very few Norwegians who knew of the Trolls' existence.

The King growled, grunted and roared. Munsen translated quietly that the King was displeased with Ingrid. The King had ordered her to keep these humans away from the chamber for several days. Why had she brought them here? Why had she not obeyed her King? Did she want to take his place? Did she want to be King? Ingrid fell to her knees, grovelling for forgiveness. She thought the humans, weak and unwell and did not want to have them die before she could deliver them to his Majesty, the King.

The King paused and looked at her. She continued to beg for forgiveness. The King stared at her for a while longer, then he raised his arm, flipped his hand and growled commands. Ingrid sat upright, her head turning left and right, her eyes wide with panic. Two giant Trolls dressed in blood-stained leather thongs stumped forward and lifted the poor creature. She wailed, but the King ignored this, and the rest of the Trolls jeered the action. She was raised and dragged from the room.

Ham looked at Munsen, who he could see even in the yellowish light of the torches had turned a pale green.

Without turning his head to the team, Munsen muttered, "Don't eat the meat at the banquet when it's offered." Talya, Paterson and Berland turned to look where the prisoner had gone. They could still hear her cries. Munsen, who knew how cruel the Trolls could be, continued to stare at the King.

The King turned his gaze to the team.

"Why did you bring this animal with you?" he asked, looking at Major. "Is it for food?" The Troll King tilted his head as he examined the dog.

"The dog is a member of my team. He is under my protection, but he is also my protection."

"This little wolf? Hah! What can he do!" the King laughed.

"Major, angry face." The king leaned forward and then sat back quickly.

"Metal teeth! I like it. Truly a warrior. Maybe I will not eat him."

"You will not eat him, your Majesty."

"You are in my land, in my chamber Captain Hamilton. "Yes, I remember you from when you visited the old King many years ago. And you, Captain Munsen, from your visit not so long ago to the court of another of the older Kings. You would be wise not to threaten me; this is my court and my Kingdom," the King said in what he imagined a sweet voice. It just came out as a grating growl.

"I did not come here to threaten or to damage the relationship between our tribes. I came here to talk." The King sat back in a relaxed manner.

"I have many other things to do. You will be taken to a place where you can rest until later. We shall have a banquet in your honour. We will talk then or maybe even later."

"Your Majesty," Ham interjected, "you know why we are here. May we see the Elf women before the banquet? The Elf King sent this Elf woman to see her sisters." The King looked at Ham for a while as if considering. Without replying, he grunted some commands, and the team was led away.

The escort tried to separate the team into two rooms, but Munsen insisted they remain together by speaking the Troll language.

"If they can get Talya or Major into a small group, we may not see them again."

There was no door to the cave, but many Trolls patrolled outside the cave entrance.

"I would suggest we eat some of our MREs[51] , believe me; you will not want to eat what they are offering at the banquet, although banquet is a bit too grand-sounding for what they will

---

[51] MRE – Military jargon, Meals Ready to Eat.

be serving. Ham, needless to say, the King has taken a liking to Major, whether as food or entertainment, I can't say, keep him very close to you. I suggest we eat and rest, 'later' to a Troll could be hours or days, I suspect days. There is no daylight here, so time is only a vague concept. Eat, rest, and I'll take the first shift. Talya, I don't want you taking a shift on your own, not because you are a woman, but because you are a potential target. Double up when you are awake." Munsen looked over at Major. "You too, Major." Major raised his eyebrows and looked at Ham. Ham laughed and rubbed behind Major's ears. "You agree with that, Ham?"

"One hundred per cent. You go ahead, Magnus. I'll take the third shift. The rest of you sort yourselves out." Ham leaned into Major and whispered in his ear, "you stay with me. Rest now, boy." Ham wondered how Macduff and the rest of the team were getting on.

Room Service

Paterson nudged Ham out of his light slumber. At the same time, Ham felt Major, already awake, stir. Ham had a feeling that he knew what was going on. Ham sat up and felt around with his hand and quickly found his hand-held Dragon SR FTS Thermal Sight night vision. Switching the device on, he scanned the entrance to their cave and the rest of the teams. He saw everyone preparing similar devices, some were handheld, and others mounted on their weapons. The weapons having been previously loaded and locked[52] and requiring only the release of the safety catch, the teams watched, aimed and waited.

Scanning back to the cave entrance, Ham saw two Trolls sticking their heads around the door. Having lived most, if not all, of their lives, in the labyrinth of caves, the Trolls' large eyes had adapted, and they could see in the dark better than the humans; not clearly, but better. The Trolls had little regard for the puny overground warriors, but their King had told them to sneak in surreptitiously.

---

[52] Unlike the Hollywood, Lock and load, which does not make sense.

These creatures did not carry out any activity without the direction of the King; to do otherwise was to invite yourself to appear on the menu.

But what the Trolls did not understand was that these humans and their weak above-land vision were enhanced with the thermal imaging equipment. The humans could see the creatures clearly as a few of their big dirty-green friends tried to sneak in. The lumbering creatures, to their credit, entered and started to move around the cave soundlessly. Three headed to where Talya had lain earlier. She had silently changed position slightly to 'welcome' the Trolls. Two crept towards Ham, but he knew that he was not the target. The King wanted Major.

They could have switched on some light and exposed the intruders, but Ham and Munsen had already agreed to a plan of action should such an intrusion occur. They had to make a show of strength; otherwise, the Trolls would disrespect them and would again attempt to try further nocturnal activities during their stay.

Ham's thought was to kill the creatures with suppressed fire, causing confusion as the creatures died from an unknown cause. In discussion with Munsen, this was discounted, and maximum firepower and noise were decided as the best option.

Laying down the night vision device and moving a hand to restrain Major so that he did not get in the way, Ham opened fire at the nearest Troll with his pistol. The signal sent; the rest of the teams opened fire, lighting the enclosed space with flashes. With his Dragon mounted on his rifle, Paterson made short work of the two Trolls heading their way. Munsen, Talya and Berland dealt with the other three. It was a massacre.

"What now, boss?" asked Paterson.

"We dump them outside the entrance and go back to sleep."

"Won't they want revenge or try again?"

"They don't think like us, John. Their King sent them in on a whim. They were cannon fodder. He doesn't care what happened to them. Remember, he's the smart one. He probably thought something like this might happen. We'll dump the bodies outside as we would garbage. They'll pick them up when they're ready."

"And then?"

"Some Trolls will be spitting out lead bullets during their next meal, I guess."

"Geez," muttered Paterson.

"John, they came to take Talya and Major. If they had succeeded, Talya would be the King's plaything for a while, and when he was bored, she would have been passed on down the chain. Major would probably be restrained somewhere and brought to fight bears or wolves for their amusement."

Ham switched on a torch which lit the gruesome sight. He surveyed the five dead Trolls scattered around the cave.

"Ok, I'm an old man and a lieutenant general, so you, young fit and healthy lower ranks can take the trash out. Sergeant Major Berland, when you have done that, would you be so kind as to make one of your excellent coffees. I'll take the next watch. Rest while you can. I don't think they will be back for a while. Well done." Ham smiled at the group, who glared back. Ham held his weapon on his lap. He knew the Trolls could be unpredictable and attack again at short notice. It was best to be safe.

Munsen and Berland grabbed the legs and dragged the blood-covered green body.

Talya and Paterson did the same, but with more grunting. In the end, the pair dragged the body out in jerky tugs. Munsen and Berland did the same for their second bundle. Trolls were heavy.

"I have got to get myself one of these 'Lieutenant Generalships'," Munsen muttered out loud as he strained to carry the deadweight. Ham grinned but continued to watch the doorway.

A Little Touch of Bad Memories

Ham had stood guard a couple of rotations without incident when he felt rather than saw, Major moving. At first, he thought he was just chasing rabbits, as he liked to call it. Major would often enact running or playing in his sleep. This time like others in the past was different. Major was in distress.

Major had served as a Special Forces War Dog in Iraq and Afghanistan. He had been trained to sniff out explosives, and people and attack when ordered.

During his last tour in Afghanistan, the team had been ambushed, and his dog handler had been mortally wounded. Major had defended his handler during the firefight, fighting off several Taliban fighters. In the process, he had received wounds in several places, including his jaw. Even as he could not bite the attackers, he had scratched and clawed at them to protect his handler.

The team found him dying, bleeding to death on top of his handler.

With other team members wounded in the ambush, the team leader had aborted the mission, and they were all casevaced[53] by helicopter to the nearest medical facility. All the team, including Major, were stabilised before being passed back for major surgery. Major and two other team members were flown back to RAF Brize Norton for further treatment.

Major's body wounds were treated, and he received a metal jaw, upper and lower, to replace his damaged set. It took him a long time for his body to recover and even longer for his mind. But like any warrior that has lived through a traumatic experience, he had PTSD[54]. His PTSD did not seem to bother him often, he could go months without an attack, but it was usually as he slept when it came. Ham knew this was one of these occasions. All Ham could do was cuddle, hold, and stroke Major while whispering gentle words. It didn't matter that the dog did not understand; it was the reassuring tone that mattered.

"You and me both, mate. We'll get out of this business as soon as we can. There's a good boy. Good lad."

---

[53] casevaced – casualty evacuated
[54] PTSD – Post Traumatic Stress Disorder.

Munsen came over, and Ham explained. Munsen stroked Major and went to check on everyone else.

After a while, Major calmed, woke, snuggled up to Ham, and slept.

Ham thought about his own PTSD. He did not have nightmares or seizures; he internalised, swallowing the memories and fears. Ham thought he had coped very well with it, but the general had noticed, and he had retired Ham from the department, only to bring him back years later when he was needed.

Paying the Late-to-Be King a Visit

After forty-eight hours of waiting in the pitch dark and fighting off a second kidnapping attempt, Ham had had enough. Ham and Munsen had envisaged this scenario back in Narvik and had planned for it. They held a quick council of war with the rest of the team and prepared and checked their equipment. It was time to take control of the situation.

John Paterson led the way out of the cave, towards the King's court, following the track laid from the fluid dripped from his rucksack on their way into the complex. Invisible to the naked eye, it glowed bright green when viewed through their night vision equipment. They did not encounter any Trolls enroute but found the King's audience chamber packed as before. The King wanted his audience.

All eyes suddenly turned towards them as they entered unannounced. Even the all-knowing King seemed surprised, then annoyed.

"I did not summon you! What are you doing here? Go back, and I will summon you when I am ready to see you. I have not come to a decision yet. Go!" he commanded.

"Your Majesty, we came here in good faith to ask you to return the Elf women that your Trolls have kidnapped. You have attacked us. You have kept us waiting, but we will not wait any longer."

"And what will you do, little man. There are thousands of my subjects and only five of you. What can you do? Now, I have decided, the women stay, and you will die." He sneered and then laughed aloud. The laughter grew from near the King and grew like a wave as it spread.

"I thought that might be your answer." Ham looked around. "Yes, there are thousands of you, but…" looking back at the King. "Only one of you." The King did not seem to comprehend straight away, even after Munsen repeated Ham's words in the Troll language.

"Ok, do it," Ham said in an even tone.

Johansdotter shot the guard on the King's right, Berland the guard on the King's left, and Paterson, the King. Each shot struck a forehead. Even with their thick skulls, each fell instantly, dead. In the silence that followed, Munsen spoke in Troll.

"We came in peace for the Elf women that you stole. Your foolish late King tried twice to steal this woman warrior and this dog belonging to this man. This man is a King and a blood brother to the Elves, and he does not like when Trolls steal his things. He does not like it when Trolls steal his blood brother's things. We shall now return to the room that you made us wait, and we shall wait twelve of our hours. I know that you do not understand our time, so I will place this here, in the centre of this hall. Those of you close enough will see that it has two hands and will see that they move. When they both return to their same position, the device will explode, demolishing not only this cave but the entire network of caves. Every one of you will die in the explosion."

"You will die as well, Major Munsen!" a voice shouted in Norwegian from the shadows. Munsen translated for Ham.

"Tell me something I don't know, Mr Nilsen," Munsen replied.

"So, you know who I am, Major," Nilsen responded, stepping out of the shadows. Berland stood beside Ham, translating for Ham and Paterson. "I think we can correct this little misunderstanding."

"I don't think there is any misunderstanding Mr Nilsen. You have the contract to deliver cattle and sheep to the Trolls in exchange for precious minerals and gems, which you can retain. For this privilege, you pay a tax to the government. There are rules to this contract, of course. You cannot sell the Trolls alcohol or weapons, both of which you have been doing. You are not allowed to accept oil in payment, again, something you have been doing. You are allowed a maximum staff of five, but the number in your compound is fifteen at the last count. This is an above-top-secret arrangement, and the number of people to be made aware of the Trolls' existence must be kept to a minimum. One final thing Mr Nilsen, we know it was not the Trolls who captured the Elfin women, but your men. You sold the women to the Trolls."

"Prove it!" shouted Nilsen.

"The fact that the King's bodyguards have automatic rifles is part of the proof. The Elfin women will confirm what I have just said about their capture. Lastly, we have been watching you. I think you are going to jail for a very long time, maybe forever. Or an insane asylum. It's not my choice. Because of the secrecy, I'd guess at the latter."

Munsen shook his head as if he were so sorry. "Twelve hours is when the hands are in the same position. You have twelve hours to choose a new King and bring all the Elf women to this room. Only twelve hours. As some of you can see, the hands have moved already." Munsen turned to go but turned back. "This device will explode if any one of you goes near it or tries to move it. Please don't do that, or we shall all die." Munsen turned and walked towards the room they had waited in earlier.

Ham saw Nilsen running for a tunnel out the corner of his eye.

"What about him?" Ham asked.

"He's not going anywhere," replied Munsen calmly.

"Where did you get that crazy looking device?" Ham asked as they settled down to wait.

"It's the alarm clock from that duty room our two lovers occupied earlier and a box I found in a cupboard. Still want to play poker?"

Munsen took the first watch. They were not bothered for about ten hours.

The King is Dead. Long Live the King!

"Welcome, Captain Munsen and Captain Hamilton. I am King Mungo," the young King said in a confident voice. "Hugo did not handle the situation well. I have thought about it. Hugo took the Elf women a whim. We don't need them or want them. They are ugly and weak. I have decided that it would be better if you left and took your troublesome Elf women with you," said the new King in excellent Norwegian.

"Your Majesty is gracious and wise," replied Munsen.

Something caught the corner of his eye, and Ham turned to see twelve Elfin women in light chains escorted into the audience chamber. Ham nodded to Talya and Berland, and they went over to the women and brought them back to their group.

Ham noticed the locks fastening the chains around the captives. He looked at Munsen. Munsen caught his look and spoke with the King.

"May we have the keys to the chains?" Munsen asked sweetly.

"I'm afraid we lost the keys. Most regrettable. Hugo must have put them somewhere. I do not know where," equally as sweetly. "Would you dismantle your bomb and leave, please. We have the funeral rites for our late King to see to."

"He means dinner is being served soon," Munsen whispered to Ham. "You do realise that once we have dismantled the 'bomb' and left, we will be ambushed in the tunnels on the way out. That's why he wants the women still chained up. Easier to control." In a louder voice, he said, "Sersjantmajor Berland! Deactivate the bomb. Cut the red cable first, then the blue, and then the green. Make sure you cut them in the right order." Berland looked at the package and back to Major Munsen, slightly puzzled. "Trolls are colour blind; thank goodness they did not cut the wrong cable." Berland nodded imperceptibly, walked over and took out a Leatherman multipurpose tool. He carefully snipped the red cable, the red cable and the red cable. Berland could almost hear the King breathe a sigh of relief as the last cable was cut. Berland carefully picked up the package and returned it to Munsen's rucksack.

Munsen thanked the King and refused the kind offer of an escort through the maze of tunnels. They left into a tunnel behind them.

Paterson led the way, using his night-vision goggles to follow the track left by the fluid he had dripped a couple of days before. Munsen followed him, scanning the joining tunnels, nooks and dark recesses. Talya followed, leading the Elfin women. Ham walked with the women, picking the simple locks by touch as they walked. He put each chain and lock into his bergen as he freed the Elf. Bringing up the rear, Berland covered their rear.

Ham concluded that the thin chains must have been magical because when they were released, the woman changed quickly and noiselessly into the wolf form, their ragged clothes left discarded on the floor. Even the female of the species, Elf wolves, are larger than nature's natural wolves. They are more dangerous; whereas a wolf is cunning, Elf wolves are intelligent. Ham could see that Major wanted to join the wolves, but Ham ordered him back beside him. The larger wolves could deal perfectly well without Major's help. Major seemed disappointed.

Ham could hear the wolves' claws scratching on the rocks ahead. The Trolls setting the ambush somewhere ahead were in for a surprise.

Ham released the last of the women. She changed into a wolf and lopped off after her Elfin sisters as he put the chains into his bergen. Talya remained in human form and moved closer to Ham. She reckoned that they had enough teeth and claws ahead of them; her assault rifle with night vision was probably a better choice covering the dark shadows leading off the sides. If the Trolls snubbed out the flaming torches, they would need three-sixty vision.

Race to the Surface

"Magic chains? They are thin but surprisingly tough and seemed to hold the women captive in human form." Ham asked Talya as they moved along the tunnel, scouring the dark corners for hidden Trolls.

"Well, yes, you could call them that. The Dwarves made them during the Elf-Dwarf War. The Dwarves discovered an alloy that stops Elves' ability to transform. The Dwarves made chains, nets even manacles out of the alloy. As you say, very strong. I don't know how the Trolls got hold of the chains. The Dwarves and Elves are not exactly on friendly terms. Knowing the Trolls, they probably stole them."

"Would the Dwarves sell them?" Ham asked. Talya snorted.

"Not to Trolls." She paused. "Definitely not to Trolls."

"Would they sell to anyone else?"

"You know the Dwarves. Give them enough shiny gold money, and they will sell you anything."

"You mean they would sell to humans?" Talya thought about it.

"Maybe, but it would be for a huge amount of money, and that still does not answer how the Trolls had them."

"Yes," said Ham thoughtfully.

As Talya and Ham moved forward, they came across Paterson and Munsen. Ham looked at Paterson quizzically.

"You're not leading the way," he said, stating the obvious. It was Munsen who replied.

"There is not enough room at the front. Twelve hairy-arsed wolves, excuse me, Talya, do not need our help heading for the fresh air. God help any Troll who gets in the way. We would have got to the surface if we'd followed the drips, but our furry friends upfront are taking the direct route. Just follow them, and we'll be out in no time." Following the wolves was easy; they howled, they growled, they slathered. Ham could hear their claws on the rocky floor. Occasionally, he heard a cry, a scream, and although he could not swear to it, the tearing and ripping of flesh. Shortly afterwards, they would come upon a bloodbath of flesh, bones and blood.

"John, I would advise you not to upset your future wife," Ham whispered.   Paterson nodded slowly.

Ham could smell the fresh air; it was colder but cleaner. Suddenly, there were gunshots ahead. It was primarily automatic fire, too much for Ham's liking. They heard the cries of the wolves and the yelps and screams of pain.   The operators ran forward to investigate. In a large cavern that Ham remembered was near the entrance lay several elves, blood pooled near their corpses. Ham realised almost immediately that Nilsen had summoned help from the compound and planned to remove any witnesses.

Ham took in the scene and shouted, "They're from the compound. Nilsen's men. Talya tell the Elves to stay undercover. Major Munsen, you take charge. Paterson, you assist. I'll cover our backs." Munsen looked back down the tunnel.

"There are no Trolls there," he stated, puzzled.

"Yes, good, aren't I?" Ham smiled. Munsen shook his head and called his team forward. Paterson nodded to Ham and joined them. Ham wanted to be at the front, guns blazing, but he realised that he had moved into the realms of management and that whether he liked it or not, there were younger, fitter, better-qualified operators to do the action hero stuff.

Paterson picked off one or two shooters while Munsen's team accounted for another couple, but there were still another ten or eleven ambushers by Ham's judgment. Another single shot rang out over the cacophony of fire, and it dropped to nine or ten.

Suddenly the automatic gunfire increased dramatically, different weapons, and then stopped entirely as quickly as it had risen.

"Boss, you there? It's Macduff and the lads. We seem to have some dead men in front of us. I do hope they were not ours."

"Talya, quickly tell your Elves that Macduff and her team are friends!" Talya called out in a surprisingly soft voice in a language that Ham had never heard before. The wolves emerged as Ham realised that he had not told Macduff that the wolves were Elves and were friends. "Macduff, the wolves are friendly! The wolves are on our side!" Luckily no one was shot or bitten.

Ham and the others walked past the dead elves, now in human or Elf form, and plain old dead humans to join Macduff, Rob and Jaimie. A wolf howled in the distance.

"No Croig?" Ham asked.

"No, boss. I thought it better to leave him in Largs. I'll explain later. All's good, though. No problem."

"Boss, just as we came in, I saw one man take off into the woods towards that compound," Rob stated.

"Yeah, running like the clappers he was. Dark curly-haired, glasses, carrying an assault rifle," Jaimie added. Ham looked at Munsen. Munsen looked at Berland, and Berland took a radio handset off the shoulder of his bergen. Berland spoke only a two-word code, nodded to Munsen and Ham and replaced the radio handset onto his bergen. Macduff looked quizzically at Ham.

"Major Munsen has just ordered an assault by another Norwegian team on the compound. Sadly, there will be no survivors. The contractors all knew the rules when they signed the contract and broke them big time. Most of them were illegally employed by the compound manager, Nilsen. They would have known it was illegal but highly paid work. They took their chances and lost. A case of terminal stupidity."

"Oh," said Macduff.

"He won't make it," Ham said quietly. The British and Norwegian teams turned to look at him. "Nilsen," Ham continued. "He won't or didn't make it to the compound, did he, Talya?" The eyes moved from Ham to Talya, who shrugged. "com'on folks, we all heard the wolves howling." Ham looked at Talya. "Your father?" She nodded.

"Father, uncles, cousins. After arranging the kidnapping of the Elf women, and the death of those killed in the ambush, I don't think my father would be in a forgiving mood," Talya stated matter-of-factly. "I would say he is already dead." Paterson glanced sideways at Ham. Ham ignored him.

Munsen nodded to Berland, who called in the helicopter. Both teams climbed on board, and they flew back to Narvik.

Narvik

While Munsen debriefed the team in the main room over coffees, Ham took Macduff to the duty room. He offered her a seat. She made to sit on the rumpled but comfy looking bed.

"Er, I wouldn't sit there if I were you." She looked at him puzzled and sat on the hard wooden chair. "Trust me," he stated, closing the matter. Ok, tell me about your day."

Macduff knew he wanted to know what had happened since he left Largs a couple of days before.

"We picked him up when the ship docked. When he left to go home, we followed very discreetly. It's all happy families. Daddy comes home; kids are happy to see him, lots of squealing and laughter. We could hear it. He gets a meal from his loving wife. Smelt good. He goes upstairs and has a shower. We could hear him singing in the shower, good voice, and see the steam coming out the vent; he likes it hot. I imagine he puts the kids to bed or kisses them goodnight. Anyway, we pick him up at the door again, he kisses his wife and off he goes down the pub. Drives he does, silly man, taking a risk driving to a pub. Anyway, he goes to the pub; I saw him go to before. We follow him in, Janet, Megyn and me as one group and Rob and Jaimie in the other. No sign of Croig at that point. We watch him mixing and mingling. It's his local, and he's well known there. We sit separately from the boys. Jaimie goes to the bar to order drinks; I send Megyn with Janet. That way, Megyn can get near the fisherman. Janet was right; the Princess came back complaining that he stank to high heavens of deodorant, or aftershave, or perfume. Jaimie had more of a problem; you see, he was propositioned a few times at the bar and on the way back with Rob's drink. You see, it was a gay bar. Our fisherman swings both ways."

Ham laughed out loud because it was unexpected.

"Sorry, carry on. What happened next?"

"Well, Megyn lost interest big time, not because the lad had a family or was gay; Janet said Mermaids don't care about that kind of stuff; she just couldn't stand the smell of him. She said it made her want to gag."

"And then?"

"Mission complete. The Little Princess lost interest in Prince Charming straight away.

We finished our drinks and left. It seemed Rob was willing to stay awhile, but Jaimie couldn't get him out the door quick enough. I think our Jaimie might be a bit homophobic, and Rob finds that amusing."

"Good, that's the Princess, and the fisherman sorted. Next, the Vampires."

"Mr Croig arrived the next morning, a bit stunned and bewildered. One minute he's a rising star in MI6, and the next, he has been given the old heave-ho for following orders. Kicked out on the streets, you might say. He's a bit bitter, to say the least. If he's faking it, he's damn good. Anyway, I've put him in Ives' room at the safe house for the time being. We'll have to work something out before Steve gets back." Ham nodded. Macduff continued," That afternoon, we kitted up and headed for the hills, well, the Highlands. We went to the first bothy on the list. The boys went in and made themselves comfortable, while the ladies made themselves as comfortable as could be expected outside, in the December cold, freezing our butts off. We got ourselves a nice little spot, near enough to come to the boys' rescue should they be attacked by the Baobhan Sith, but far enough away to avoid detection. The boys appeared to be drinking and in a merry mood. They played music and exclaimed the desire for women. Nothing. The night drew on, and I was beginning to think that we'd have to move on the next day and try another bothy."

"Yes," encouraged Ham.

"The next morning, as the sun rose, we all got up. Lying in front of the bothy door were two women's heads."

"What? Heads? As in decapitated heads?"

"Yes. Everyone was a little shocked, I can tell you, except Megyn. She didn't bat an eyelid. A tough cookie that one." Ham looked thoughtful for a moment.

"So, the Baobhan Sith sorted their problem and left us a message to let us know."

"I reckon so. We cleared up our mess and left it at that. We drove back to Largs."

"What did you do with the heads?"

"We left them where they were. I reckon the Baobhan Sith will take care of their own. If not, somebody's going to get on Hell of a shock when they turn up at that bothy."

"Give Ms Miller a call and ask her to ask the police nicely to check that the area is clear.

Better they deal with it rather than civilians. But as you said, the Baobhan Sith probably took the heads back. Ok, when you got back to Largs, what then?"

"Megyn has no experience of weapons, so she'd be no good to us here. If she is going to be part of the team, she will need a lot of training. Croig is an unknown factor. I don't know what he's been trained on weapon-wise. I don't know; he could be all vodka-martini stirred, not shaken, I don't know. Anyway, I thought it best to leave him to get settled in. There's no water here, so I thought it best to leave Janet in charge of the other two. A quick call to Ms Miller, and here we are. I tell you that bed looks mighty tempting. You have no idea how cold it was on the ground last night." Ham saw her shudder involuntarily with the memory. Another thought came to her mind, and she smiled. "Croig and Megyn seem to be getting on fine. I may have forgotten to mention to him that she is a Mermaid. That bed sure looks good. Do we have time?"

"Ah no, wait until you get back to your nice comfy bed. You'll appreciate it more. A couple of quick questions; you said there were only two heads? You had a look around in case an animal moved one?" Macduff nodded in reply.

"Yes, boss, just the two."

"Did you check the teeth?" Ham asked. Macduff looked uncertain.

"No, should I have? What was I looking for? Ah yes, the Baobhan Sith are Vampires. Sorry boss. Problem?"

"Nothing we can't fix. Go back in with the others and ask Rob and Jaimie if they checked the teeth. Let me know when I come out. And could you send John in, please?"

With a 'Yes boss', she was off.

A few moments later, there was a knock on the door, and John entered. "Boss?"

"John, when we get back, I want you to get a few things, either bought local or from Ms Miller. We'll talk later. You will need some simple camping equipment as well. For three people, you, me and mister Croig. You'll need his measurements; I don't think Ms Miller will have them yet. Try to pick stuff with little or no metal. It's only for a couple of days, so don't worry about it breaking. I'll need to talk to the birds, but I suspect we will have to go hunting. You won't need any guns or anything with metal. No Rambo knives or bug-out belts[55]or whatever you call your escape belt. Oh, and load up some good dance music, you know, the seventies and eighties stuff, on a phone or something small, but that can play the music out loud. Right, let's see how the others are and get on our way home."

---

[55] Bug-out belts – belts with survival equipment always worn by Special Forces in case the have to 'bug out', or leave in a hurry.

A Double Murder

"Lieutenant General Hamilton, my, you have risen quickly through the ranks," the Guardian cooed in her Caribbean lilt. "I guess you have come to collect the Princess. We have had long chats while you were away. She says you do not give her enough treats. She says Major gets more. And something else, I think. What can I do for you, mister Hamilton?"

She took out the sleepy Princess from the folds on her woollen cloak. Princess saw Ham and, turning her head pouted.

"She's glad to see you but upset that you left her behind," the Guardian said. Without a word which was unusual, Princess climbed into the rucksack Ham proffered, and Ham replaced it onto his back. Ham could feel Princess making herself comfortable.

"I need to talk to the birds," Ham said simply. "I need to know what's going on with the Baobhan Sith. I think someone or something is playing games."

"Oh, I can answer that. The Chieftain did try one last time to sort out the problem. The three rogue Baobhan Siths ambushed and killed the Baobhan Siths sent to persuade them to return to the fold. The rogues removed the heads and stuck them outside the bothy where your team tried to lay a trap for them. They thought that this might make you believe that the Baobhan Sith had dealt with their own, and you would leave them alone, at least for a while. The three are still in that area, and the Baobhan Sith Chieftain would like you to deal with them." Ham nodded thoughtfully.

"Why don't the Baobhan Sith deal with their own? Why do they want us to do it?"

"What the three are doing is what Baobhan Sith used to do in the old days waylaying strangers and feeding on their blood. As per the contract, your law and your rules say they cannot do this anymore. The Chieftain feels that, as they have broken your law, not theirs, you should punish them."

"What about the two Baobhan Sith that they killed? Isn't that against their law?" The Guardian shrugged.

"That puzzles me a bit; I'm sure the Chieftain said that three were sent to negotiate. Maybe animals moved the third head. Anyway, as far as the assassination or execution goes, they want you to do it," she said firmly, "You see, one of them is the Chieftain's daughter."

"Oh, sweet Jesus," Ham groaned.

Ignoring him, the Guardian continued, "The Chieftain's daughter is headstrong and led the other two on their killing spree. If she is not dealt with, others will follow her in the old ways. The Chieftain knows what must be done, but as I'm sure you understand, does not want to do it or order it be done."

"Great, so we are to be the assassins," muttered Ham. Aloud he said, "Ok, my team will deal with them." Ham shook his head slowly and muttered very quietly to himself, "There has been a lot of killing recently."

"Yes, but necessary, the Troll King was taking his Trolls down the wrong path and that evil man, Nilsen, and his minions could not be allowed to live with the knowledge they held." Ham stared at her; he had not realised that he had muttered loud enough for her to hear and certainly did not understand how she knew of things that had just happened in Norway. She smiled at him, turned and left.

Sisterhood

That night the men made merry or at least looked as if they did. They drank or appeared to drink copious amounts of whisky.

Bothies do not have running water, sewage or electricity; if you want water, you bring your own unless there is a nearby stream. If you're going to pass motion, you go outside to relieve yourself away from the stream; solids you bury with a shovel. As for electricity, you light a fire for heat and bring batteries for everything else.

They had no visitors despite proclaiming the desire for women, another prerequisite for a Baobhan Sith visit, similar to the Hollywood Vampire myth that Count Dracula must be invited into a house.

They took turns on guard. Three figures appeared at the open doorway during Ham's early morning watch. One stepped brazenly forward. She wore a long green dress that hung from her feminine frame. Her dark hair hung over her shoulders, catching the breeze coming through the door. Ham looked down and saw a hoven foot peeking from beneath the dress.

"Sorry, we missed the party. Did you miss us? Your trap was so simple. Did you think that you could trick us? Your colleagues tried. Fools! We left them a message," as she spoke, the other two came in behind her and stood on either side of the doorway. One had jet black hair and the other a dark nut-brown like the speaker. All three were attractive with a determined, slightly arrogant manner. They wore no makeup, but their natural beauty shone through. Ham was surprised that when they smiled, it was pleasant and endearing. Their teeth were straight and even and very white, Hollywood white. He glanced at her hands, slim and ladylike, devoid of nail varnish, but the nails were well maintained.

"You should have come earlier; we could have had a good time," said Ham nodding towards the empty whisky bottles and iPod with speakers. Paterson and Croig had risen by this time and stood to either side of Ham. The Chieftain's daughter tilted her head a couple of times and studied the room silently, intensely.

"You have no weapons; I sense no metal, no iron; how were you going to kill us?"

"We came to talk, to persuade you to return to your clan and not kill any more people. You know the treaty signed with your people. You leave us alone, and we will leave you alone."

"Weeklings. Contracts and treaties are for weaklings. The Baobhan Sith used to rule these mountains and glens; we took what we wanted. Who are you little man to think that you can control our ancestral right?" She stepped forward; the others followed. Ham held up his hands as if he could push them back.

"Stop! This is your last chance! Go back to your people." A sneer passed across the leader's face. The sneer turned grotesque when her face transformed. The pretty green eyes turned yellow and animalistic, her nose flared, her teeth suddenly grew, transforming into upper and lower fangs. They were long, curved and sharp. At the same time, her hands grew claw-like, with her delicate fingernails transforming into talons. They stepped forwards again, fully aware of what their change of appearance would do to any victim. Their arms raised to grab. Ham stepped back, and as one, the three men drew their ceramic knives from their concealed sheaths and slashed at their opponents' necks. Ceramic knives are not suitable for stabbing; they are sharp but brittle, you would likely end up holding a broken blade, wondering what to do next. All three men held two knives each. The white blades did not register with the Vampires; they were surprised when the razor-sharp blades slashed and cut their skin on arms, faces, necks and torsos. It was three against three, talons and teeth against knives, boots, and when a blade snapped, hands. The fight was ferocious, slashing, grabbing, dodging. As Ham fought the leader, he realised that the three men might lose. He knew he dared not risk a look, but it was a hard-fought fight judging by the grunts, growls and roars.

She lunged with one hand while attempting to slash with the other. Any time she came close enough, her teeth gnashed towards his neck. Ham pushed her back with his one free hand; one broken blade dropped long ago in the m☐l☐e. Ham panted with exertion, awaiting the new attack.

Suddenly a taloned claw gripped an opponent's neck from behind. The Baobhan Sith's hands flew to the claw to try to release it. Seeing his chance, Ham slashed at the exposed unprotected portion of the neck and cut deeply. Blood shot out in a high-powered spray from the wound. A high pitch cry emitted from the leader's fanged mouth. Then she gargled, and blood spewed from her mouth. The claw that held the neck released its grip, and the leader fell. In her place stood another Baobhan Sith, looking equally grotesque in her Vampire form.

"Take her head while she is weak, or she will recover!" the creature called as she moved over to the Vampire fighting Croig. She similarly grabbed the Baobhan Sith and dug her talons into the neck. Croig stepped back in shock.

"Kill her now, man!" she shouted above the noise in a Highland accent. Croig slashed at the Baobhan Sith's torso. "Her neck, you fool!" Croig did as he was told. As the Baobhan Sith fell to the ground, he, too, reluctantly started to decapitate his opponent.

Paterson's opponent had stopped fighting when she heard the call from the fourth Baobhan Sith. Paterson, too, stopped fighting, not knowing what was going on. He looked at his opponent, who was backing off, to the fourth Baobhan Sith, who was moving towards her, to Ham. Ham was busy removing the leader's head. Croig was doing the same to his opponent, but more hesitantly, as if he was waiting for someone to tell him to stop.

"Why did you stop?" the creature called to Paterson. Paterson turned from his opponent, who had transformed back into the dark-haired female. She looked frightened as she saw the fourth Baobhan Sith approach.

"No! I only followed. I did as Morag commanded. I didn't want to. She..." Her voice gargled as the Baobhan Sith grabbed her pretty neck with her clawed hand.

"Kill her! You must kill her. I cannot."

"Do it!" commanded Ham rising from his completed grizzly task. "It has to be done." Paterson slashed, and the girl-like figure gurgled to the floor. Paterson stood shocked. "Remove her head, or must I do it!" Paterson knelt and carried out his task.

When Ham looked up from what Paterson was doing, he saw that the fourth Baobhan Sith had transformed back into her feminine form. She nodded when Paterson was finished. She turned and looked at Ham.

"You may leave the carcasses here; we shall take them and give them proper burial rites. I will tell my mother that the task is complete. The status quo is restored." Ham pointed at the body at his feet.

"Your mother? This was your sister?" Ham asked, pointing at the body of the leader.

"Yes," she replied simply, turned and left, leaving three slightly stunned men behind.

"I'm surprised you didn't try to recruit her boss," Paterson commented.

"Damn! You're right. I hadn't thought of that." After a moment's pause during which he had started to pack his gear, he continued, "What about her cloven feet? You can't walk around Largs with cloven feet, can you?"

"Boots," interjected Croig. "A specially designed pair of boots could hide them." Croig continued to pack his gear. Ham looked at him and realised that Croig might fit in quite nicely.

"John, if you are getting married to Talya, I can arrange for you to swop into the Norwegian team for a while or her to swop over to ours. What do you think?"

"I think I'd prefer to think about my matrimonial arrangements somewhere else," he replied, pointing at the decapitated bodies lying nearby.

"We could give them mister Croig for Talya," suggested Ham to Paterson. "I'm sure he would love to live in Bod□ for a while." Croig looked up and across at Ham. Ham, his face blank of emotions, calmly packed his gear.

Croig, Daniel Croig rolled his eyes and slowly shook his head.

Printed in Great Britain
by Amazon